Arthur Upfield

DEATH OF A LAKE

A division of HarperCollins*Publishers*

To Mr James L. Hole

Editorial Note

Part of the appeal of Arthur Upfield's stories lies in their authentic portrayal of many aspects of outback Australian life in the 1930s and through into the 1950s. The dialogue, especially, is a faithful evocation of how people spoke. Hence, these books reflect and depict the attitudes and ways of speech, particularly with regard to Aborigines and to women, which were then commonplace. In reprinting these books the publisher does not endorse the attitudes or opinions they express.

AN ANGUS & ROBERTSON BOOK

First published in 1954 by William Heinemann Ltd
First published in 1956 in paperback by Pan Books Ltd
This edition published by Collins/Angus & Robertson Publishers Australia in 1991

Collins/Angus & Robertson Publishers Australia
A division of HarperCollins Publishers (Australia) Pty Limited
Unit 4, Eden Park, 31 Waterloo Road, North Ryde NSW 2113, Australia

William Collins Publishers Ltd
31 View Road, Glenfield, Auckland 10, New Zealand

Angus & Robertson (UK)
16 Golden Square, London W1R 4BN, United Kingdom

National Library of Australia
Cataloguing-in-Publication data:

Upfield, Arthur W. (Arthur William), 1888-1964.
Death of a lake.
ISBN 0 207 16274 3
I. Title.

A823.'3

Cover illustration by Russell Jeffery
Printed in Australia by Griffin Press

6 5 4 3 2 1
96 95 94 93 92 91

1

Lake Otway

LAKE OTWAY WAS dying. Where it had existed to dance before the sun and be courted by the ravishing moon there would be nothing but drab flats of iron-hard clay. And then the dead might rise to shout accusations echoed by the encircling sand dunes.

The out-station crowned a low bluff on the southern shore, and from it a single telephone line spanned fifty miles of virgin country to base on the great homestead where lived the Boss of Porchester Station, which comprised eight hundred thousand acres and was populated by sixty thousand sheep in the care of some twenty wage plugs, including Overseer Richard Martyr.

There wasn't much of Richard Martyr. He was short, dapper, wiry, every movement a hint of leashed strength. His face and arms were the colour of old cedarwood, making startlingly conspicuous his light-grey eyes. Always the dandy, this morning he wore well-washed jodhpurs, a white silk shirt and kangaroo-hide riding-boots with silver spurs. Why not? He was Number Two on Porchester Station, and this out-station at Lake Otway was his headquarters.

Martyr stood on the wide veranda overlooking the Lake, the Lake born three years before on the bed of a dustbowl, the Lake which had lived and danced and sung for three years and now was about to die. The real heat of summer was just round the corner, and the sun would inevitably murder Lake Otway.

Short fingers beating a tattoo on the veranda railing, Martyr gazed moodily over the great expanse of water shimmering like a cloth of diamonds. It was a full three miles across to the distant shore-line of box timber and, beyond it, the salmon-tinted dunes footing the far-flung uplands. To the left of the bluff, the shore-line curved within a mile; to the right it limned miniature headlands and tiny bays for four miles before curving at the outlet creek, where could be seen the motionless fans of a windmill and the iron roof of a hut named Johnson's Well. When Lake Otway was dead, that windmill would be pumping water for stock, and perhaps a man or two would be living at the hut six hundred rolling miles from the sea.

The cook's triangle called all hands to breakfast. Martyr again puckered his eyes to read the figures on the marker post set up far off shore. He had seen the figure 19 resting on the water; now he could see the figure 3. Only three feet of water left in Lake Otway. No! Less! Only two feet and ten inches. Were there a prolonged heat-wave in February, then Lake Otway wouldn't live another five weeks.

The men were leaving their quarters to eat in the annexe off the kitchen. The rouseabout was bringing the working horses to the yard. The hens were busy before the shade claimed them during the hot hours. The chained dogs were excited by the running horses. The crows were cawing over at the killing pens, and a flock of galah parrots gave soft greetings when passing overhead. A city man could never understand how men can be captivated by such a place . . . six hundred miles from a city.

Martyr turned and entered the dining-room, large, lofty, well lighted, and sat at the white-clothed table to eat alone. He could hear the men in the annexe, and Mrs Fowler, the cook, as she served them breakfast. Then he looked up at Mrs Fowler's daughter.

'Morning, Mr Martyr! What will it be after the cereal? Grilled cutlets or lamb's fry and bacon?'

She was softly-bodied and strong and twenty. Her hair was the colour of Australian gold, and her eyes were sometimes blue and sometimes green. Her mouth was small and deliciously curved when she was pleased. But her voice was hard and often shrill.

'Cutlets, please, Joan. No cereal. Plenty of coffee.' Noting the set of her mouth, he asked: 'A war on, this morning?'

'Ma's in one of her moods.'

Tossing the fine-spun hair from her broad forehead, she departed as though trained to walk by a ballet master, and he remembered she had walked like that one morning when the Lake was being born, and she was just seventeen, and the Boss had come close to dismissing her and her mother because she could be dangerous . . . among men without women.

'What upset your mother?' he asked when she was placing the covered dish before him.

'Oh, one thing and another.'

'You haven't been nagging, have you?'

She moved round the table and stood regarding him with eyes he was sure were green. She lifted her full breasts and lightly placed her hands against her hips, and he knew that to be a wanton a woman needed no training.

'A girl never nags, Mr Martyr, until she's married.'

'I believe you, Joan. Go away, and don't annoy your mother.'

'Well, she started it.'

'Started what?'

'Oh, nothing,' she said, and walked from the room rippling her bottom like a Kanaka woman.

Martyr proceeded with his breakfast, which had to be completed at a quarter after seven. Mother and daughter were constantly warring about nothing which came to the surface for men to see. As cook and housemaid they formed a team the like of which Lake Otway had never known. The food was excellently prepared and the house managed expertly. The main cause of contention between these women, Martyr shrewdly guessed, was their closeness in age, for the mother was still young, still vitally attractive, retaining that something of wantonness she had bequeathed to the girl. The husband? No one knew anything of the husband.

Martyr recalled Lake Otway on his accepting the appointment. The Lake was dry then, and the domestic staff comprised a man cook and the black wife of one of the hands. The house was merely a place to sleep in; these two quarrelling women gave it life.

When he was entering the office the telephone rang twice. The call would be for George Barby, who cooked for stockmen at Sandy Well, midway between the main homestead and the out-station. Martyr seated himself at the desk and filled a pipe, and had applied a match when the telephone rang thrice . . . the Lake call. He counted ten before taking up the instrument.

'Morning, Dick!' spoke a deep, tuneful voice.

'Morning, Mr Wallace.'

'How's the Lake this morning?'

'Two feet ten. Gone down an inch since yesterday afternoon.'

'H'm! No sign of rain, and Inigo Jones says we needn't expect any till March 18th. Feed still going off?'

'Within a couple of miles of the Lake, yes. Rabbits in millions. More 'roos, too, this last week than I've ever seen. Moving in from the dry areas. White Dam is down to four feet.'

'Better shift those hoggets, then,' advised the Boss. 'In fact, Dick, we'd better think of shifting a lot of sheep from your end to the Sandy Well paddocks. When the Lake goes, it'll go quick. The last foot of water could dry out in a day. It did last time, I remember. We lost two thousand ewes in the Channel that time. What d'you intend doing today?'

'I'll send Carney out to ride White Dam paddock. And MacLennon to Johnson's Well to make a report on the mill and pump and tank.'

'Better get Lester to go along with Mac, and remind 'em to lower a light down the well before they go down. The air will be foul after all this time.'

'All right, Mr Wallace. What about the horses? Any sight of a breaker?'

'Yes, I was coming to that,' replied the Boss. 'Feller here now, wanting breaking work. Good references. I'll send him out tomorrow on the truck. Let me know tonight what you want out there.'

'The breaker, is he to have a free hand?'

'As he'll be working on contract, yes. Feed with the men, of course. The name's Bony.'

'Bony what?'

'Just Bony. Talks like a uni' professor. Queenslander, I think. When you've drafted off the youngsters for him, better send all the spares in here. We'll put 'em in the Bend. Well, I'll ring again tonight.'

The line went dead, and Martyr replaced the instrument and reached for his wide-brimmed felt. On leaving the office at the side of the house he faced across a two-acre space to the men's quarters. Backed by a line of pepper trees to his right stood the store, the machinery and motor sheds, the harness room, the stable for the night horse, and beyond this line of buildings were the stock and drafting yards, the well and windmill, and the pumping house. The hands were waiting at the motor shed for orders.

There were seven men ... five white and two black. The aborigines were flashily dressed, the white men content with cotton shirts and skin-tight trousers which had been boiled and boiled until all the original colour had gone with the suds.

The overseer called a name, and one of the aborigines came to him and was told to ride a paddock fence fifteen miles in length. The other aborigine he sent to see that sheep had not huddled into a paddock corner. A Swede, who had been unable to conquer his accent despite forty years in Australia, he sent to oil and grease a windmill, and a short, grey-eyed, tough little man named Witlow he despatched to see if cattle were watering regularly at a creek water-hole. Carney, young, alert, blond, smiling, was sent to White Dam to note the depth of water again. There was left MacLennon, dour, black-moustached, dark-eyed and with a prognathous jaw. A good man with machinery.

'Want you to look-see over Johnson's Well, Mac. You'll have to take the portable pump to lower the water in the shaft. Get the well pump out and inspect. Have a go at the mill, too. Make a note of everything that needs replacement. The truck will be coming out tomorrow.'

'Just as well. The ruddy Lake won't last much longer by the look of her, Mr Martyr.'

'And send a light down the well before you go down.'

'Oh, she'll be all right.'

'That's what the feller said up on Belar,' Martyr coldly reminded MacLennon. 'That well is still all right, Mac, but the feller who went down without testing five years ago has been dead five years. You'd better take Lester to give a hand. Use the ton truck. I'll tell Lester to draw your lunches.'

Lester was coming from breakfast and Martyr met him. He was middle-aged, shrivelled like a mummy by the embalming sun and wind. He affected a straggling moustache to hide his long nose. His pale-blue eyes were always red-rimmed and watery, and he was cursed by a sniffle which deputized as a chuckle. A good stockman, a reliable worker, for the time being Bob Lester was acting homestead rouseabout, doing all the chores from bringing in the working hacks early to milking cows and slaughtering ration sheep at evening.

'Morning, Bob!'

'Mornin', Mr Martyr!' The watery eyes peered from under bushy grey brows.

'Not up your street, Bob, but would you go with Mac to Johnson's?' Without waiting for assent, Martyr concluded: 'Draw your lunches, and give Mac a hand with the portable pump. By the way, the breaker will be coming out tomorrow.'

Lester sniffed.

'Tomorrow, eh! Do we know him?'

'I don't. Goes by the name of Bony. A caste, from what the Boss implied. Ever hear of him?'

'No ... not by that name. Them sort's terrible good with horses when they're good, and terrible bad when they're crook.' Lester claimed the truism. 'You giving him an off-sider?'

'Haven't decided,' replied the overseer, abruptly distant, and Lester sniffled and departed to ask Mrs Fowler to provide lunches.

Martyr strolled to the shed housing the power plant and started the dynamo. From there he crossed to the stock-yards, where the men were saddling horses. The night horse used by Lester to bring in the workers was waiting, and Martyr mounted the horse to take the unwanted hacks back to their paddock, a chore normally falling to the rouseabout. On his return, he assisted MacLennon and Lester to load the portable pump and saw they had the right tools for the work at Johnson's Well, and after they had driven away he went into the house and stood for the second time this morning on the front veranda overlooking Lake Otway.

Although Richard Martyr was acknowledged to be a stock expert and a top-grade wool man, it had been said that he didn't seem to fit into this background of distance and space bared to the blazing sky, but, in fact, he fitted perhaps a little too well. Moody, Mrs Fowler said of him; deep, was the daughter's verdict. A psychiatrist would have been assisted had he known of Martyr's secret vice of writing poetry, and could he have read some of it, the psychiatrist might have warned the patient to resist indulgence in morbid imaginings.

Even the coming dissolution of Lake Otway was beginning

to weigh upon his mind, and his mind was seeking rhyming words to tell of it. Actually, of course, he was too much alone: the captain of a ship, the solitary officer of a company of soldiers, the single executive whose authority must be maintained by aloofness.

Because he had watched the birth of Lake Otway, he knew precisely what the death of Lake Otway would mean. He had watched the flood waters spread over this great depression comprising ten thousand acres, a depression which had known no water for eighteen years. Properly it was a rebirth, because Lake Otway had previously been born and had died periodically for centuries.

Where the 'whirlies' had danced all day, where the mirage had lain like burning water, the colours of the changing sky lived upon dancing waves, and the waves sang to the shores and called the birds from far-away places ... even the gulls from the ocean. Giant fleets of pelicans came to nest and multiply. The cormorants arrived with the waders, and when the duck-shooting season began in the settled parts of Australia the ducks came in their thousands to this sanctuary.

All that was only three years ago. Nineteen feet of water covered the depression three miles wide and five miles long. Then, as a man begins to die the moment he is born, so did Lake Otway suffer attrition from the sun and the wind. The first year evaporation reduced the depth to fourteen feet, and the second year these enemies reduced it to eight feet.

It was the second year that Ray Gillen came over the back tracks from Ivanhoe way on his motor-bike and asked for a job. He was a wizard on that bike on all kinds of tracks and where no tracks were, and he was a superb horseman, too. Even now the sound of his laughter spanned the ridges of time since that moonlit night he had gone swimming and had not returned.

He ought to have come ashore. It was strange that the eagles and the crows never led the waiting men to the body, for there were exceptionally few snags in Lake Otway, and no outlet down the Tallyawalker Creek that year.

If only a man could strip that girl's mind and forget her body. She used to catch her breath when Ray Gillen laughed, and when he teased her, her eyes were blue ... like ... like blue lakes.

The Golden Bitch!

2

Bony comes to Porchester

IT WAS NOT an event to be forgotten by those closely associated with it. The details were recorded by the police and studied by Detective-Inspector Bonaparte many months later.

Ray Gillen arrived at Lake Otway on September 3rd, and the next morning was taken on the books by Richard Martyr. As is the rule, no questions were asked of Gillen concerning previous employment or personal history, the only interest in him by his employer being his degree of efficiency in the work he was expected to do. And as a stockman he was certainly efficient.

Nine weeks later, on the night of November 7th, Gillen was drowned in Lake Otway, and late the following day the senior police officer at Menindee arrived with Mr Wallace, the owner. To Sergeant Mansell Martyr passed all Gillen's effects, he having in the presence of witnesses listed the contents of Gillen's suitcase and the items of his swag.

At that time the men's quarters were occupied by Lester, MacLennon, Carney and George Barby. The quarters consisted of a bungalow having three bedrooms either side of the living-room. Lester occupied one room and MacLennon another. Carney occupied the same room with Gillen, and Barby had a room to himself.

November came in very hot and the men often descended the steps cut into the face of the bluff and bathed in the lake, which at this date was twelve feet five inches deep. Neither Lester nor MacLennon could swim. Barby could, but never ventured far from the shore. Of about the same age ... twenty-five ... both Gillen and Carney were strong swimmers, especially the former, who boasted that, with a little training, he would swim across the lake and back.

On the night of November 7th the moon was almost at full. The day had been very hot, and the night warm and still. The men played poker, using matches, until a quarter to eleven, when they went to bed. Carney stated that shortly after he and

Gillen got to bed, Gillen announced his intention of going for a swim. Carney, on the verge of sleeping, declined Gillen's invitation to accompany him. He stated that it wasn't until he awoke the following morning that he discovered Gillen hadn't returned.

The last Carney saw of Gillen was when he put out the light on leaving the room. Gillen then was wearing only his pyjama trousers. A quick check of Gillen's clothes proved that he could not have returned from the lake, slept, awakened early and dressed and gone out. It was after breakfast, when Martyr appeared to give his orders for the day, that Gillen was reported missing.

For Sergeant Mansell a routine job. He examined Gillen's clothes, his swag of blankets, and the contents of his suitcase, the suitcase being of good quality. There was no clue to Gillen's people. He examined the man's motor-bike, a powerful machine in good condition, noted its registration and engine numbers, and went back to his office.

Wallace and his overseer organized the hands. Aborigines were brought from the River, and meanwhile Lester and Carney and MacLennon scoured the country about the Lake in the extremely unlikely event that Gillen had wandered away and become lost.

On the third day, and subsequently, all hands patrolled the shores to await the coming in of the body. The wind direction and the currents set up by the wind were carefully calculated. But the body did not come ashore, and it was ultimately assumed that it had been trapped by a wire fence crossing the lake which was, of course, submerged when the depression filled with water.

Among Gillen's effects was neither a driver's licence nor a registration certificate for the machine he rode. It was learned that the registered owner of the motor-cycle was a timber worker in Southern Queensland. He was traced to Toowoomba, where he was living at a good hotel and spending freely. He said he sold the bike to a man named Gillen, and described Gillen. He said that his present state of affluence was due to having a half-share with Gillen in a lottery ticket which won £25,000.

Asked how the money was divided, the timber worker told of an agreement to draw the full amount in cash from the bank into which the cheque for the prize had been paid. In an hotel room they had portioned out each share in Treasury notes. They wanted to look at a lot of money, and Gillen had left the next morning on his bike, saying he intended to tour Australia.

And the extraordinary facet of this tale of luck and division of so large a sum in notes of low denomination was that it was true. Gillen had left Toowoomba with something like £12,500 in his possession.

When his effects were examined first by Martyr in the presence of Lester and MacLennon, there was no money.

All the banks in the Commonwealth were asked if an account in Gillen's name had been opened. Result negative. Gillen's journey south into New South Wales and still farther south was traced. Here and there people remembered him. Debonair, handsome, a man seeking adventure. Plenty of money? Well, no, he didn't give that impression. What had the timber worker said of Gillen? 'Money! Ray never cared a hoot for money. Twelve thousand odd in his kip wouldn't worry him.'

Questions: Had he arrived at Lake Otway to accept a job when he possessed twelve thousand pounds? Again according to the timber worker, it was likely. Significantly, the timber worker added: 'Ray would take a job anywhere where there was a "good sort" around.'

There was a 'good sort' at Lake Otway. That £12,000 could not be traced. Gillen was known to be an excellent swimmer. The statements of four men tallied in that they all played poker with Gillen and always with matches. Fifteen months after Gillen was thought to be drowned, Inspector Bonaparte happened to peruse the case file.

There were several angles which, although unusual, were by no means psychologically improbable. Firstly, the personality of the man Gillen. He had been born and educated in Tasmania. On leaving school he worked on an uncle's farm, but the farm, apparently, was too cramped, and the boy crossed to the mainland, where he passed from job to job until, as a stockman in Northern Queensland, he had volunteered for service in Korea, where he had completed his term of service. Returning to Queensland, he joined two men in a timber contract.

After leaving the Tasmanian farm, there had never been lack of money in Gillen's life. The sudden acquisition of a large sum of money did not cause Gillen to rush to the fleshpots, as it had done to his partner in the lottery ticket. That lucky ticket provided Gillen with additional means to freedom, and many a man wants just that.

Therefore, that Ray Gillen had stuffed about £12,000 into his kip and set off on a motor cycle to see Australia was in keeping with the psychology of many young men in Bony's experience. Again, in accordance with the known personality of the missing man, Bony was confident that Gillen had asked for a job at Lake Otway after and not before he had met the 'good sort'. It had been the girl and not the job which decided Gillen to seek work at Lake Otway.

There arose the inevitable doubt when a strong swimmer takes a swim shortly before midnight and is drowned, and has among his possessions a large sum of easily spendable cash. A telegram to the senior officer of police at Menindee produced a result which could be looked at from several points. The Sergeant replied that none of the people employed at Lake Otway left after Gillen was drowned. Then no one of those employed with Gillen could have stolen his money, for surely had one done so he wouldn't stay on, but leave to enjoy the spending of it. But the fact that not one person *had* left was also decidedly odd, for all of them save the overseer could be typed as members of the great floating population who seldom stay in one place for more than a year.

And so, fifteen months after Gillen was assumed drowned, Inspector Bonaparte climbed into the cabin of a three-ton truck in the guise of a horse-breaker, Sergeant Mansell and Mr Wallace, the owner-manager of Porchester Station, being the only persons aware of his identity.

The horse-breaker was smoothly dressed in brown twill shirt and trousers, well worn elastic-sided riding boots, and an old broad-brimmed felt. And on the load was his neatly rolled swag of blankets and normal equipment. The truck driver wore a patched pair of greasy grey trousers, a blue denim shirt, whiskers seven days old and no boots. He was twice Bony's weight and one inch shorter. The Boss had referred to him as Red Draffin.

Once clear of the homestead paddocks and the obstructing

gates, Bony rolled a cigarette and settled for the long run. The sun this day of late January was hot and the air was clear. Bony was home, and the simple people like Red Draffin are at home here, too. Red trailed a shower of sparks from his pipe by knocking it against the outside of the door, and said:

'So you're from Queensland, eh? From old Uradangie. Long time back when I was up there. Usta be five pubs in my time. They still doing business?'

'Four are. The Unicorn was burned down.'

'That so! Hell! Remember the Unicorn. She was kept by ole Ted Rogers. Ruddy doer he was. So was his ole woman. They took turns in minding the bar ... week and week about. Neither could last longer than a week at a time. End of the week's spell in the bar, and both of 'em was a cot case. I did hear that Ted Rogers died in the horrors.'

'So did Mrs Rogers. She was in the horrors when the pub went up.'

'Was that so!' Red Draffin spat with vigour and almost automatically drove the loaded vehicle along the track twisting about low sand dunes, across salt and blue-bush flats, over water-gutters, and across dry creeks. 'Well, Ma Rogers could always drink as good as Ted, and he was extra. I seen him open a bottle of rum and drain the lot without winkin'. Hell! Men was men in them days. What brought you down south?'

'Change of country,' Bony replied. 'I get around.'

'I usta,' admitted Red Draffin. 'Never stayed on one fly-speck more'n a month.'

'You have settled down?'

'Yair. You blows out in the end, y'know. You find that the sandhill beyond the next one's just the same, and that Orstralia is just a pancake dotted with pubs wot are all alike. Course, times have changed a lot. The coming generation is too sap-gutted with fruit juices and milk in their tea, and nowadays if a man has a go of the horrors he ain't liked. Once on a time if a man didn't have the horrors he wasn't reckoned a man's shadder.'

'Had a bender lately?' Bony politely inquired.

'No, not for a long time now. I'm gettin' on, and after a bender I suffers something terrible from indigestion. Got to take a bit of care of meself.'

'How old are you?'

'Don't rightly know. Last census time, the Boss estimated me at sixty years. What d'you reckon about carb soda?'

'For the horrors?'

'No, me indigestion.'

'I've been told that carb soda is good for anything.'

''Bout right, too. Read in the paper that a bloke in Russia lived to be a hundred and forty 'cos he washed every day in carb soda. Might take that on meself. Carb soda's cheap enough.'

Bony thought the suggestion an excellent idea, but asked: 'How long have you been working on Porchester?'

'Me? Nine years and a bit. I've kinda settled on Porchester. Wallace is a good boss, and, as I said a mile or two back, the pubs in Menindee is just the same as they usta be up at Uradangie. Whisky's got more water in it and they charges six times more, that's all.'

'You'd know this run, then?'

Red Draffin spat at the passing wind, flexed his shoulders.

'I know every water-hole, every sandhill, every blade of grass on Porchester. Every ruddy sheep knows me be name, and this year there's over sixty thousand of 'em. Never took much to horses, though. You like horses . . . musta.'

'Yes, I like horses. What's the overseer like at Lake Otway?'

'Mister Martyr? Good enough,' replied Draffin. 'Knows his work. Done no one a bad turn that I ever heard about. Keeps his place and expects us to keep ours. You married?'

'Yes.'

'Me, too. Lasted eleven days and a bit. Found out me wife was married to a butcher in Cobar. She cleared out with a shearer, and me and the butcher's been good cobbers ever since. Women! You go careful with the women at Lake Otway.'

'There are women?'

'Two. Mother does the cookin' and the daughter does the housemaiding.' Draffin chuckled. 'Ruddy termites, both of 'em.'

'How so?'

'They eats into a man's dough from the inside out. And there's blokes wot likes it. Wouldn't leave the place. Reckons they got a good chance with the daughter or the mother. They sends away to Sydney or Adelaide for presents for 'em. You'll be a wake-up in no time.'

They passed a deserted hut built of pine logs, used only at the shearing season. An hour later they sighted a windmill and two huts partially surrounded by a high canegrass wall.

'Sandy Well,' Draffin said. 'Get a bit of lunch here.'

'Half-way house?'

'That's right. Twenty-six mile to the homestead and twenty-six on to the Lake. Feller called George Barby cooks here when he ain't fur-trapping. Good bloke, George Barby, though he is a pommy.'

Three dogs came racing to meet the truck and escort it to the door in the canegrass wall. From the view of the surrounding sandhills Bony deduced that the wall was essential when the storms raged.

Through the door there emerged a slightly-built man, dark of hair and pale of skin. He was wearing white duck trousers and a white cotton vest. After him came an enormously fat pet sheep, and after the sheep came two outsized black and white cats. Finally there appeared a tame galah, red of breast and grey of back. The parrot waddled forward absurdly, flapped its wings and raised its rose-tinted comb while shrieking its welcome.

The pet sheep chased Red Draffin round the truck, and George Barby said to Bony:

'Come on in and have a cuppa tea.'

3

The Thinker

FOR A MAN of sixty, Red Draffin could move. So, too, could the pet sheep. The bootless, whiskered man appeared from behind the truck and raced for the door in the wall, the large wether hard astern and bouncing the sand with legs like props. Shouting with laughter, the truck driver kept the hard, butting head at bay with one hand and with the other he thrust a plug of black tobacco between his teeth, bit off a chunk and presented it to the sheep. The sheep almost spoke his thanks and retired placidly chewing.

Throughout this exhibition, the pale-faced cook never smiled; in fact, Bony fancied he detected disapproval of Red Draffin's undignified behaviour. He led the way through the door in the wall. After him went Bony, and after Bony came Red Draffin. Following on came the two enormous cats, and after the cats waddled the galah. The dogs only remained without. The sheep arrived later.

Inside the wall of canegrass were two huts, and the cook led the procession to that which served as the kitchen-dining-room.

'Boss said you were coming out,' he remarked, waving to the table set for three. 'Did you bring me stores and mail and things?'

'Get 'em off the load later, George,' replied Draffin. 'Meet Bony. He's goin' out to the Lake breakin'.'

George and Bony nodded the introduction, and Draffin went on:

'Bony's come down from Uradangie. You never been up there, George?'

Barby asked to be told why he should have been up at Uradangie and Bony looked about the hut. It was surprisingly clean and tidy. The cooking was done with camp ovens and billies on the large open hearth. There were crevices between the pine log walls and several holes in the corrugated iron roof. But the place was cool this hot day, and what it was like when the wind blew the sand off the summits of the surrounding dunes he could imagine.

Barby served roast mutton, potatoes and tomato sauce. The bread was well baked and the tea was hot. He sat on the form at the table opposite his visitors, and the conversation at first excluded Bony. Slightly under fifty, he had been so long in Australia that his Lancashire accent had almost vanished. His face was long, his chin pointed. His eyes were dark and, in the soft light, brilliant. And like the great majority of bush dwellers he was intelligent and well read.

To Bony's amusement the galah suddenly appeared above table-level. Using beak and claws, the bird climbed the cook's cotton vest to gain his shoulder, and once there distended its rosy comb and emitted a screech of defiance at the guests. Barby went on talking as might a mother pass off the misbehaviour of her child, but the effort was ruined when the bird said softly and confidentially in his ear:

'Bloody ole fool.'

'Lake's getting low, they say,' Barby remarked, offering no sign of annoyance, or of being conscious of the 'brat'. The bird proceeded to preen his feathers, and Draffin said:

'Down to three feet. Bit under, accordin' to the Boss this morning. She'll go out like a light when she does throw a seven.'

Barby politely wiped his mouth with a pot rag, and the bird lovingly scraped its beak against his ear.

'Ought to be good money in rabbits,' he said. 'And now that Royalty's taken to fox furs the skins ought to be high come May and June.'

'Yair. But rabbit skins are low now, though. Only three quid a hundred.'

'Quantity would make the dough,' Barby pointed out. 'There's quantity enough round that Lake, and when she dies there'll be more rabbits than could be handled by a thousand trappers. I'm thinking of giving it a go. What d'you reckon?'

'Could think about it,' answered Draffin. 'You said anything to the Boss?'

'This morning. Boss said he'd try for another cook. You size up the possible take out at the Lake, and we'll decide when you come back.' To Bony he said: 'You going to work contract?'

'Yes. On a dozen horses to start with.'

The galah screeched, and the noise would have upset a stoic. Barby puffed into its near eye and the bird screeched again, and at once, insulted, proceeded to descend from the shoulder as it had climbed. It fell off the stool to the ground and nipped a cat that spat and fled. Quite unconcerned, Barby said:

'Nice place, Lake Otway. Good tucker. Good quarters. You ought to do well. Tell the women you're married and got fifteen kids, and you're hard put to it to buy fag tobacco.'

'I tipped him off,' said Red Draffin.

'I am married, and I have three children,' Bony told them. 'I can easily add another twelve. Termites, Red said they are.'

Barby regarded Bony with prolonged scrutiny.

'As I told you, Lake Otway's a nice place. Best policy is to know nothing, and see everything, and give nothing away.

Some of the fellers out there been there too long. You know how it is.'

'I have known a similar set-up,' agreed Bony. 'I'm all for the move on.'

'And we'd better get going, too,' said Draffin, rising.

All went out to the truck ... dogs, cats, sheep and galah. Draffin climbed the load to take off stores and a bag of mail and papers. The sheep nudged at Bony's hip, persisted, and the cook said:

'He wants a pinch of tobacco.'

Bony produced the 'pinch' and the sheep daintily accepted it and chewed with evident delight. The galah waddled to his feet and ducked its head and turned over on its back. For the first time Barby smiled. He clicked his tongue and the sheep went to him. He picked up the cats and placed them on the sheep, and the bird he put with the cats, and as the truck rolled away, Bony waved and was always to remember that picture.

When a mile had passed under the wheels, Red said:

'If the Boss wants to shift flocks from the back end of the run where it's pretty dry already this summer, I can't see him agreeing to George taking on the rabbits. Cooks ain't that easy to get. If the Boss says no, George might stand by it, but I don't think so. For a long time now George has had his mind on trapping when the Lake dried out. Funny bloke.'

'How so?' pressed Bony, turning his sea-blue eyes to the driver.

'Well, he don't spend and he don't drink and he don't go for skirts. They sez never to trust that kind of bloke, but George is all right even though he's got a mania for saving money. Now me, I reckon money's only good for booze. But what does George do? He saves his dough till he's got enough to buy a good ute and a trapping outfit. When fur prices is good he slings in the cookin' and goes trapping, and when the trappin' is finished he goes back to cookin'. No between spell, no guzzle on the honk. Not even a trip down to the city. Why? Search me! Tain't like he was savin' to buy a pub, or a race-horse or something. He ain't got no wife to drain him, neither. Leastways he never owned to one.'

The wind came after the truck and the cabin was hot and fouled with burned gas and oil. Only at Sandy Well had they seen animals on this trip, and the naïve would have complained that the land was a desert. Invisible animals hugged the shadows of trees and bush, and deep underground the warrens were packed with rabbits.

They were travelling over a treeless plain extending for twelve miles when Draffin broke a long silence.

'Crook, the Lake dryin' up like she is,' he said as though speaking of one close to him. 'Lot of fish in her, too. Cod up to nine pound and brim up to seven.'

'The floods filled it, of course,' encouraged Bony.

'Yair. Record flood what began up your way. The River got miles wide, and the overflow brought water into the Lake. Nineteen feet of water she took, and with it she took enough fish spawn to feed Orstralia for a year.'

'And now the water has drained from the Lake?'

'No. Evaporation took six or seven feet a year. Then there's the birds. Ruddy thousands of birds from pelicans down to moorhens. And this summer there's been millions of rabbits drinking at her. Cripes! No lake could stand for that.'

'Do any fishing yourself?'

'Now and then.'

'Boat, of course.'

'There was a boat, but she broke up on the beach one windy day. You hear about the bloke what was drowned? In the Adelaide papers?'

'No, I didn't read about it. Working for the Station?'

'Yair. Bloke by the name of Ray Gillen. Goes to bed a hot night and then says he'll go for a swim. Good swimmer, too. Usta go a hell of a way out and muck about before he came in. Boasted he'd swim across the Lake and back. Could swim, all right, but he got himself drowned. About eleven at night, it was. Full moon. Left the quarters with only his 'jama trousers on. Never came back.'

Yet another gate stopped them, and after Bony had opened and closed it, and they were moving towards scrub-covered dunes which appeared an impassable barrier, he said:

'The body was recovered?'

'No, it wasn't,' replied Draffin. 'There was no body come ashore, no 'jamas, no nothink. Ray Gillen just went for a swim and the next morning they wondered wot in hell had happened to him. Got blacks out from the River. Scouted around for a week. They tracked him down to the water but couldn't track him out again. They nutted out the wind and drift of the tide and such like, and argued Gillen had to come ashore along the west end of the Lake. But he didn't. He stopped right down on the bottom somewheres. Funny about that. I always thought there was . . .'

'What?' Bony softly urged, and it seemed that the noise of the engine prevented the question from reaching the driver. Louder, he added: 'What did you think?'

'Well, just between us. Tain't no good stirring up muddy water, but I've always thought there was something funny about that drowning. You see, Ray Gillen wasn't the sort of bloke to get himself drowned. He was the sort of bloke wot did everything goodo. Fine horseman. Make you giddy lookin' at him ride his motor-bike. Swim like a champion. Goes through Korea without battin' an eyelid.'

'And nothing has been heard or found since?'

'Right, Bony. Not a trace. Trick of a bloke, too. Always laughin' and teasin'. Good-lookin' and a proper skirt chaser. The young bitch out there was eyeing him off and puttin' the hooks into him, but I reckon he was too fly for her. Anyhow, bad feelin' worked up with the other blokes, and one evening there was fireworks, Ray and MacLennon getting into holts. I wasn't there, but Bob Lester told me they hoed into it for half an hour before Mac called it a day.'

'But Gillen must have been drowned,' Bony argued. 'Wearing only his pyjama trousers, he couldn't have cleared away to another part of the State.'

'That's so,' Draffin agreed.

'Well, then, he must have been drowned,' persisted Bony, prodding the simple driver to defend himself.

'Could of been, and then he could of not. George Barby told me he reckons Gillen went after a woman that night.'

'Wearing only pyjama trousers?'

'It was a hot night, and it ain't necessary to be all dressed up.'

'Well, he went visiting, then disappeared. That it?'

'Yair.'

Red Draffin braked the truck on a hard claypan and silently cut chips from a black plug. Without speaking he rubbed the chips to shreds and loaded his odorous pipe and, still without speaking, lit the pipe and again settled to his driving. When they had covered a further three miles he voiced his thoughts.

'Don't know what you think about things, Bony, but I reckon booze is a safer bet than women. You can trust booze. You know just what it can do to you. But women! All they think about is what they can get out of a bloke. Look! Only the blacks get their women in a corner and keeps 'em there. Do they let women play around with 'em? No fear. They gives their women a beltin' every Sunday morning regular, and there's never no arguing or any funny business during the ruddy week.'

'There's an old English custom. Are you sure the blacks choose Sunday mornings for the belting?' Bony asked, and Red Draffin, noting the smile and the twinkling blue eyes, roared with laughter.

'Could be they makes it Sat'day night sometimes so's not to miss out,' he conceded, a broad grin widening the spaced flame of hair on his face.

'What makes you think Gillen mightn't have been drowned?'

'Well, you being a stranger, sort of, I can talk to you, and you can keep it under your bib. As I said, it's no use stirring up mud. When you get a bird's eye view of Ma Fowler and the daughter you might feel like me about Ray Gillen. Y'see, it was like this. Ray had a good suitcase, and one day I'm having a pitch with him in his room when he was changing his unders. He pulls the case from below his bed, and he unlocks it with a key what he kept on a cord with a locket, what he always had slung round his neck. The case was full of clothes. He took a clean vest and pair of pants off the top of the stuff in the case, and he had to kneel on the lid to get it locked again.

'That was a week before he went missing. I wasn't at the Lake when he drowned, if he did, but George Barby was, and the next day, or the day after, the overseer got Bob Lester and George to be with him when he opened the case and made a list of what was inside. And accordin' to George Barby, the case was only three parts full of clothes and things. I never said nothink to no one except George about that, but I've thought a lot of what happened to make the tide go down like it did.'

'And did the overseer discover anything in the case, or find anything about Gillen's parents or relatives?' Bony asked, to keep the subject before Red Draffin.

'Not a thing. Ray's motor-bike's still in the machinery shed 'cos nobuddy's claimed it, and the police took the suitcase and things. I'll tell you what I think. I think Ray got wise to them women, or someone got wise to him, and that sort of started someone off. I tell you straight, I don't believe he got himself drowned, and I wouldn't be surprised if they come across his skeleton when the Lake dries up and find there's bones broken what the water couldn't of broke. So don't go muckin' about these women. Keep to the booze and you'll be all right, like me.'

'I will,' Bony promised, and there was no further opportunity to discuss the disappearance of Ray Gillen.

So swiftly as to provide a shock, the ground fell away before the truck, to reveal the track winding down a long red slope, the buildings clustered at the bottom, and the great expanse of sun-drenched water beyond, shaped like a kidney and promising all things delightful after the long and arid journey.

'Beaut, ain't she!' remarked the ungainly, uncouth driver, and added with genuine regret: 'Just too crook her going to die.'

4

'I am what I am'

THE TRUCK STOPPED outside the store and Bony's world was filled with sounds common to every outback homestead. Chained dogs barked and whined. The power engine chugged in rivalry with the clanging of the lazy windmill. Cockatoos shrieked and magpies chortled. People appeared and gathered about the truck.

Bony opened his door and stepped out. To him no one spoke. He saw Red Draffin pass the mailbag to a dapper man and knew instantly he was the Boss of the out-station. The other men were types to be seen anywhere beyond the railways. He was conscious first of a big-boned woman with flashing dark eyes and raven hair, and a moment later was gazing into eyes as blue as his own. In them was reserved approval. His eyes registered points ... deep gold hair, oval face, wide full-lipped mouth ... and again his eyes met the eyes of the girl, and they were green and smiling and approving.

'Now you two wash and come in for your dinner,' the elder woman told Red Draffin. 'I've kept it hot for you, so don't delay by gossiping.'

Draffin grinned at her, and took Bony to the men's quarters where they shared a room. In the shower house at the rear of the building they washed and then Bony needs must return to the bedroom to comb and brush his hair.

'Never mind making yourself look like a fillum star,' Red said.

Bony was sure that neither comb nor brush had been applied to the red hair for many years, but his own lifelong habits could not be interrupted by Red's impatience. He was conducted across the open space and into the men's dining annexe off the kitchen. Mrs Fowler appeared carrying loaded plates.

'Well, how's things, Ma?' Draffin cheerfully asked as he slid his enormous buttocks along the table-flanking form.

The woman's dark eyes flashed and her mouth became grim.

'You should have been smothered at birth.'

'Now, now, no offence meant,' placated the driver. 'All widders are natural mothers to me. You're a widder, aren't you? Hope so, anyhow.'

'Eat your dinner. And don't waste your time. I told you last time you were out that you haven't a chance.'

'So you did. Never mind. Next time I'm out here you won't. Or it might be the time after.'

Mrs Fowler sat on the end of the form nearest the door to the kitchen and regarded Bony with slow appraisement. He was supposed to be a horse-breaker and to be casual in manner and careless in speech, but he was too wise to adopt in the beginning idiosyncrasies which with the passage of time would be difficult to maintain. As, ultimately, he would be judged by his acts, he decided to be himself.

From glancing at the man of cubic proportions and slovenly habits he studied the woman. That she was the mother of

Green Eyes was very hard to credit, for there was no hint of the matron about her figure. She smiled at Bony with her lips and not her eyes.

'D'you think Red would have a chance, Mr ... er ...?'

'Call me Bony,' he replied, beaming upon her, and noted the fleeting shock he gave. 'I cannot believe that Mr Draffin has the merest ghost of a chance.'

'Chance of what?' asked Joan Fowler, who appeared at the kitchen door and came to sit opposite her mother. She sat slightly sideways, that she could the better see Bony who was sitting on the same form.

Bony hesitated to explain, and was glad when Red took the lead.

'The chance of marrying your mother, Joan. What do you reckon?'

The smoky blue-green eyes were insolent and the girl smiled. 'Not a hope, you would never be able to fix her.'

The mother rose hastily, saying:

'That's enough of that.' Then she looked at Bony, her dark eyes casual, but incapable of masking her mind. 'You'll like being here, Bony,' she said. 'How long are you staying?'

Although returning her gaze, he was conscious of the girl's eyes.

'It depends,' he replied. 'A month perhaps.'

'Where have you come from?' asked the girl.

'Down from Uradangie,' Red gave the answer. 'Up at Uradangie women never arst questions.'

'You hurry with your dinner, Red, and get out,' Joan told him.

'I'm not leaving without Bony,' Red stated. 'I like him too much to leave him alone with you two.'

'Bony can look after himself,' snapped Mrs Fowler.

'Not with you, he can't. He ain't old enough yet to hold his own with either of you.'

Mrs Fowler gathered the plates on a tray and departed to bring in the sweet course. Red winked at Bony, and tore a crust of bread with teeth able to smash walnuts. The girl watched him, a sneer on her face, and determined to 'sit' him out. Her mother reappeared to ask:

'Do they bake better bread up at Uradangie, Bony?'

'Madam,' Bony gravely began, 'neither at Uradangie nor

elsewhere in Australia do they bake better bread than yours. And, please, permit me to compliment you on your cooking.'

The woman's smile of appreciation was almost tender, and then Draffin intruded.

'Talks like Ray Gillen, don't he?'

The smile was wiped from the woman's face.

'He does not, Red Draffin,' she said, venomously.

'Something like,' purred the daughter. 'We are going to like him, too.'

Bony almost bowed sitting down, and Draffin had to toss in the final spanner.

'Well, well, it won't be long now 'fore the Lake dries out and we can collect poor old Ray and find out if he did die from no air. Wouldn't be surprised if . . .'

'Stop that kind of talk, Red,' commanded the elder woman.

'All right! All right! Don't go crook at everything I say,' complained Red and lurched to his feet. 'Come on, Bony. Let's go 'fore there's blood spattered all over the walls.'

'Do you play cards, Bony?' asked the girl. 'Come over one evening. You'll be welcome.'

'Thank you. Yes, I like a game of poker now and then.'

'I like poker, too,' the girl said, sleepy green eyes challenging alert blue eyes. But Bony smiled at both women and followed Red Draffin out into the sunset.

Red introduced him to the other men, and they were not greatly interested, superficially, in the stranger. The two blacks had withdrawn to their own camp, an old hut farther along the lake shore, and the whites were excusably engrossed in their mail and papers, which were irregularly delivered. He felt their reserve and decided it was too soon to worry about the precise classification of their attitude. The only man with whom he had conversation was called Earle Witlow, middle-aged, rotund, grey and cheerful, and the subject of mutual interest was horses. Another, elderly but alert and addressed as Swede, invited all and sundry to play cards and received no co-operation. He didn't meet Martyr until the following morning when orders were issued for the day, and by then he had summed up this small community.

The two aborigines, of course, were a section to themselves. Earle Witlow and the Swede appeared to be joined in some kind of alliance, and the remainder were peculiarly individualistic. These individualists were Lester, MacLennon and Carney. They were the 'old hands', who, with George Barby, had been working here when Ray Gillen was drowned.

MacLennon and Carney were sent out for the youngsters and half an hour later their whips could be heard like exploding rifles, and soon a spear of dust speeding down the slope to the homestead became a river of horses, and ultimately the head of the spear was rammed into the open gateway of a yard. They emitted a cloud of red dust for a minute or two before the restless animals quietened.

Men sat on the top rail of the yard and watched the horses – the overseer and Bony, Lester and MacLennon and Carney. No one commented, and Bony quickly felt he was being appraised rather than the youngsters.

Fifteen taut-eyed young horses who had never known bridle and saddle, or the caress of a rope, stared at the men on the rail, and the men rolled cigarettes or filled a pipe and waited. They would have to be satisfied that he, Bony, could break in horses, for they must be made to accept him as such, and so enable him to fit into their own background.

Without being a horseman one could watch the change from the exhilaration of the open gallop, to the uneasy fear of the trap which held them, to the acceptance of the trap and men immobile on the top rail. And then when Bony slid to the ground within the yard, fifteen pairs of eyes pricked and fifteen pairs of nostrils whistled wind.

Martyr and his three stockmen moved not a fraction. Their faces were blank, but their eyes were quick and hooded, as though eager to detect errors. And although he hadn't handled horses for years, Inspector Bonaparte fancied he could disappoint them.

Standing in the centre of the yard, he clicked his tongue, and the horses could not choose a corner where they might be safe. He sauntered after them as they rushed from corner to corner, deliberately taking time to judge their points and sum up their characters. For a little while he leaned against the yard rails and slowly rolled a cigarette, like a man unable to make up his mind which horse to back for a race. He put on a good act, but at the same time shrewdly chose the animals most amenable to begin with.

Then with slow deliberation of all movement, which is the greatest weapon in the breaker's armoury, he opened a gate to an inner yard. A bay filly made a hesitant step forward, hoping that through that gate lay freedom. A black sister nudged her, and as one the fifteen sprang for it. Twelve got through before the gate barred three.

With the patience of a row of Jobs, the rail-sitters watched for thirty minutes Bony merely sauntering after those three horses, round and round the yard walls. They could hear his tongue clicking, and the seemingly careless slapping of hand against a thigh, and they watched as the three animals slowly tired and became bored with this seemingly endless roundabout.

When Bony finally stood in the yard centre, the three horses also stilled to watch him, ears thrust forward, nostrils quivering. He moved quietly towards them, talking softly, and they stiffened and shivered and whistled through pink-lined nostrils. Then they would break and rush to another corner. The watchers lost count of the number of 'tries' before one horse stood, forefeet braced, nostrils flaring, muscles trembling, and waited for man's next movement.

Bony walked to this horse, his eyes upon the eyes of the horse, his voice low, crooning, himself creating the impression of irresistible power. The horse became as of hewn marble. The gap between it and the man narrowed till but two feet separated them. The horse couldn't back, for the yard wall was hard behind it; it could lunge forward, but it didn't dare. Instead, it brought its soft muzzle towards the man, and its body seemed to lean forward over the braced forelegs.

'He's hypnotizing the bastard,' hissed Lester to the overseer, and Martyr ignored the comment.

Bony's right hand rose slowly to touch the animal's jaw. The horse shivered violently. The human hand slid from the jaw to the rippling shoulder muscles, and the watchers witnessed fear die away and muscles gradually calm. They saw Bony patting the shoulder, slip a hand under the horse's throat, pass up the arched neck to the ears. Then Bony slowly turned his back to the horse, remained in that position for half a minute before walking away.

The second horse proved more difficult, but the third was like the first. and finally Bony climbed the rails to sit beside the overseer, and roll a cigarette. No one spoke. Having applied a match to the smoke, Bony said:

'You have a handy paddock for the mokes?'

'Yes. What do you think of them?'

'Passable. I'd like the lot taken out to the paddock and yarded again this afternoon.'

'Why?' asked Martyr. 'You've got 'em for the day, haven't you?'

'I want them to become used to yarding without rebellion. I want them to become so accustomed to these yards that they will never give trouble when being driven to any yard. And I want to handle them so that they will stand while I climb over them, under them, all round them. They have to be quiet before I ride them, because I'm no buck-jumper rider. I don't break a horse, I train him.'

'All right, if that's the way you want it.'

'Thanks. You might ask your riders to leave their whips behind. There's too much noise, too much excitement. Later, I'll get them used to a whip cracking against their ears.'

Martyr ordered Carney and MacLennon to return the youngsters to the paddock and to bring them to the yards again after lunch. Lester seemed inclined to remain, and was told to get on with his chores. Alone, Martyr said:

'Haven't seen you in this district before.'

'First time I've been down this way. The Diamantina's my country.'

'Oh. Then why come?'

Bony chuckled.

'Woman trouble,' he said, and from Martyr's nod knew he had been accepted.

5

Below Surface

AT THE CLOSE of his first week as horse-breaker, Bony knew he had successfully 'edged' himself into this small community, and further, he was confident that there were strange under-currents in this community, opposed to him and to two other men . . . Kurt Helstrom and Earle Witlow.

Helstrom, always addressed as Swede, was grey and tall and long-jawed. He had a strong sense of humour which he himself appreciated most and it made no impression upon his ebullient nature when others appreciated it not at all. He preferred the company of Earle Witlow to anyone else's and it appeared that Witlow liked the Swede. Witlow, much younger, looked much older, for he was a sun-dried raisin of a man who spoke but rarely to anyone other than Helstrom.

The others, that is Lester, Carney and MacLennon, for the two aboriginal stockmen were quite apart, while not openly hostile to each other were bound by an invisible cord which would have been accepted by anyone less intuitive than Bony as the clannishness of old employees.

Witlow had been employed at Porchester Station for four years, but at Lake Otway for only the last seven months, and the Swede had been put on the pay-roll eight months back. Neither had been at Lake Otway when Ray Gillen came, or when Gillen was drowned. Lester had been working on Porchester for fifteen years and he had gone to the city every year for a spell, but not after Gillen had come to Lake Otway. MacLennon's service had begun three years ago, and Carney had ridden paddocks about Sandy Well for two years before being transferred to the out-station shortly after Lake Otway had been born.

Lester and MacLennon and Carney had been working here when Gillen vanished that moonlit night. That was fifteen months back, and not one of them had left the place for a spell since then. One man of several working under such conditions of isolation might decide not to take a spell, his ambition to knock up a good cheque, but it was rare enough to be an oddity for three men to work more than a year without a holiday.

The same tag applied to the Fowler women. They had come to Lake Otway shortly after its birth and had remained ever since without once leaving the out-station. Like the men, they bought their clothes per mail-order, but, being women, it was a trifle odd how they had so long resisted the shops.

There was another matter to spur speculation. The two women, the three men and Barby, the cook, were much more concerned by the coming death of Lake Otway than seemed normal, certainly more so than Witlow and the Swede, and when Bony coloured the known facts concerning Gillen with impressions gained during this first week breaking horses he felt that the death of Lake Otway could coincide with the climax of a drama which began when Raymond Gillen came.

He had had no further opportunity to probe Red Draffin, as Draffin had returned to the main homestead the day after he brought Bony and the load to the Lake. Draffin had certainly voiced suspicions, but it had been to a casual worker who would not long remain, concerning especially the suitcase and contents belonging to the vanished Gillen. In view of the fact that it was officially believed that Gillen possessed twelve thousand odd pounds in notes of low denominations. Draffin's remarks about the 'tide' having ebbed in that suitcase appeared significant.

As Bony had foreseen, this was not an investigation wherein he could bamboozle suspects with questions and hope to bring out the solution with the slickness of city detectives backed by willing informers. Actually he had but one problem: to establish Gillen's fate, which, because of the non-location of twelve thousand pounds, cast grave doubt that the man's fate had been accidental drowning.

Seven people were here when Gillen vanished, and those seven people were still at Lake Otway, including George Barby, who was only twenty-six miles distant and who wanted to return for the trapping.

Twelve thousand pounds is quite a sum. No bank held it in safe keeping, it being reasonable to assume that as Gillen came into possession of the money lawfully there would have been no cause for him to have banked the money in an assumed name. It was also reasonable to assume that Gillen would have done something about it had it been stolen from him. Thus, until proved otherwise, it must be assumed that Gillen arrived at Lake Otway with twelve thousand pounds 'in the kip'.

Twelve thousand pounds in notes of low denomination make up quite a parcel. A bank manager had demonstrated the size of the parcel to Bony before he left Brisbane, and that parcel could be the difference between the high and the low 'tide' noted by Red Draffin.

Further, if one of the men had stolen the money from the suitcase when it was thought Gillen had drowned in the Lake, would that man have continued working at Lake Otway? Assuming so, then the reason for sticking to his job must indeed be extremely powerful.

Yes, questions here and now would be out of order. A prodding perhaps, a good deal of listening and working out sums, plus the aid of the old ally, Time, would provide a break soon or late. His role was to be unobtrusive, subtly diplomatic, acceptable to all seven suspects.

Seven suspects! The overseer, Martyr, was run-of-the-mill. Public school education . . . apprentice jackaroo . . . sub-overseer . . . undermanager. Next step up, manager. But that final step a very long step, indeed. Martyr knew how to handle men and, according to Mr Wallace, he was proficient in handling sheep and cattle. He was introspective, imaginative and ambitious.

There was Bob Lester, uninhibited, nervy, earth-bound, with a wonderful memory for sporting details. MacLennon was restrained yet virile, slightly morose, determined, and could be dangerous. Carney was young, fearless, imaginative, well read, and not as well educated as he claimed to be. Barby was something of a mystery, conforming to no type. Well read, quietly observant, careful with his money and ambitious to make more.

The women had to be considered, for either could have raided Gillen's suitcase. The mother was still young and attractive, man-hungry and avid for conquest. Not the type to stay put for so long. The daughter was alluring and knew it. Bring her in contact with a good-looking and daring young man and a bush fire could start in the centre of Lake Otway. Or would the flame be kindled by twelve thousand pounds?

It was after five in the afternoon that Bony actually came in contact with the hands, for they and Martyr had been engaged in moving several of the huge flocks of sheep from the back of the run to those paddocks around Sandy Well. Even Lester, the rouseabout, was called on to assist, so that during the day Bony was the only man about the place. He suffered but one hardship: to keep track of the lies he told, for the way of the liar is, indeed, hard.

As is the custom, one of the women would tap the triangle

with a bar to call him to morning smoko-tea and again in the afternoon. Lunch, which he took with them, was more formal. He was amused to find both mother and daughter piqued because he failed to progress according to their assessment of him.

At morning and afternoon 'smoko' they talked intelligently of everything excepting Ray Gillen, to whom he never referred, but as the days slipped by their interest in the falling level of Lake Otway sharpened. At the close of that first week of Bony's employment, the Lake fell by four inches.

The men's interest in the Lake was just as marked. Often they returned to the yards with only a few minutes in hand to wash before the dinner gong was struck, but always they scanned Lake Otway to note the imperceptible changes taking place. At this time of day, Bony was usually sitting in a broken arm-chair on the veranda of the quarters overlooking the Lake.

Then came that late afternoon when the first sign of volcanic emotion surged above surface. Bony sensed that the beginning occurred before the men returned from work, before they came trudging across from the horse yards where they had freed their mounts to roll on the sand and take their fill at the trough.

'I'm going in for breaking,' remarked Harry Carney when passing to his room. He was cheerful of voice, but anger lurked in his eyes.

'Yair, better'n stock-ridin', anyhow,' agreed Lester, and sniffled. 'You just hypnotizes a youngster for an hour or two each morning, and then lays off all afternoon in a comfortable chair well in the shade, with a book or addin' up the dough you've earned. Wonderful job.'

MacLennon, stocky and powerful, said nothing. He stood at the end of the veranda looking down at the Lake, now as placid as a road puddle. Overseer Martyr appeared on the house veranda, also obviously interested in the Lake.

'Been hot today,' Bony remarked. 'Mrs Fowler said at lunch it was a hundred and two in the pepper-tree shade.'

'Four hundred and two in the sun,' rumbled MacLennon. 'I hate these windless days. Makes the flies real vicious.'

He passed off to the shower, and the Swede came and laughed at Bony and asked how it felt to be a 'cap'list feller'

– asked with the usual roar of laughter. Witlow merely grinned and went in for his towel.

Presently Carney reappeared, cleaned and his fair hair slicked with water. He stood by Bony's chair and rolled a smoke.

'No mail out, I suppose?' he asked, gazing down at the Lake. Bony shook his head, and Carney added: ''Bout time someone brought it. Hell! The Lake looks like someone's poured gold into it.'

The gong thrummed through the heated evening air, and Bony took his old and tattered Charles Garvice to his room. On coming out, he found Lester looking at Lake Otway, as Carney and MacLennon had done, and he called:

'It will be still there after dinner.'

'Yair, that's so, Bony.' Lester joined him and they walked after the other two men. 'Going down fast, though. Another four weeks will see her out.'

'A pity.'

'Yair. She was beaut up to last Christmas, and when she was full there was no need to go down to the seaside for a cool-off beer. Given a good wind the waves would come curling in a white surf, and at night you could hear it miles away. It never seemed hot in the paddocks, when you could come home to it.'

'Have you seen this place when there's no water?'

'Too right. Just a flat all over, covered with bush rubbish. Blasted heat trap, too. Water comes into her every seventeen to twenty years, and then stays only for three years at most.'

They ate without sustained conversation, what there was of it being carried on by Witlow and the Swede. They were, of course, tired from the heat and the burning sun and the pestiferous flies, but they seemed taciturn when a normal gang could have tossed chaff at each other. Only towards the end of the meal did one address Bony, and he was Lester, who inquired of his progress with a brown gelding. Bony was making his progress report when Joan Fowler came to the door leading to the kitchen and waved to Bony, saying:

'Cards?'

Bony rose and bowed.

'At eight?' he said, smilingly.

The girl laughed and disappeared. Bony sat down conscious

of the hostility in MacLennon and Harry Carney. Witlow, the bow-legged, whimsical Witlow, dryly chuckled, and his apparent friend, the Swede, jibed:

'You tink Bony been pawing the ground whiles we's been working all day?'

'Could of been,' conceded Witlow. 'You can never trust these horse-breakers, Kurt.'

'What you reckon?' asked the Swede, grinning at Bony. 'Better for us to sit in on cards, too – just to make sure he keep all right?'

'Yair, better,' Lester put in. 'Bony isn't old enough to play cards with grown wimmen. He'd be fleeced for a monte.'

'Perhaps I shall need a little support,' Bony laughingly agreed.

MacLennon crashed his eating utensils down on his plate, got up and left. In the silence, Lester sniffled, and Carney drawled:

'You can cut out the fleecing idea, Bob. Sounds bad.'

His round face was flushed and his eyes were void of the usual good humour. The Swede leered wickedly, opened his mouth to say something and shut it in pain when Witlow kicked his ankle under the table.

That was that, and it fell out that Bony and Witlow were the last to leave the annexe. When crossing back to the quarters, the little man murmured:

'Keep your hair on, Bony. That Bitch likes to make trouble. You might be able to use yourself, but Mac's an ex-ring champ.'

'Thanks for the tip. I'll tread lightly,' Bony said, and added: 'There wouldn't be anything in treading on other people's toes here.'

'Wise feller. They're a funny mob. Best to let 'em cook in their own camp fire.'

Bony chuckled, and they paused to look out over the Lake and at the sea-gulls that came winging in to land with the hens who were waiting to be fed.

'Long way from the sea for the gulls,' Bony observed.

'Six hundred miles from the nearest salt water at Port Augusta. It could be they've never seen the sea.'

'Yes, that's likely. Get the Swede to come in for cards. Safety in numbers, you know.'

Bony pondered about Witlow, and decided he would ask this stockman a few questions.

6

Fish and Fowl

AT THE CLOSE of the first week Bony had his first horse far enough in training to be ridden outside the yard and sensible enough to be trusted to permit its rider to concentrate on matters having nothing to do with a sparkling young filly. Thus he gained freedom to examine Lake Otway, allegedly the scene of the death of Raymond Gillen. One morning he rode round the Lake, saw where the flood water had flowed into it at the northern end and where it had spilled over a sandbar into a creek at the southern end. He noted with interest the large area opposite the out-station taken over by pelicans for their hatchery and nursery, and where the swans had selected sites for their nests. Rabbits were everywhere in plague proportions, for the surrounding dunes and the slopes of the uplands outside the dunes were honeycombed with burrows. Often a 'swarm' of rabbits would dash ahead of him, and when he shouted they would burrow and he could see the sterns of animals at every hole, unable to get in for the crush. Everywhere, too, claiming every major shadow were kangaroos, and away up the slopes back of the dunes were black dots of countless emus.

A paradise for fur trappers. A mighty harvest ready for the reaping, and soon to be calcined by the sun.

Barby arrived one morning driving his utility loaded with camp gear and trapping equipment, his three dogs, two cats and the tame galah. The Boss had found another cook to relieve him, but had been unable to spare Red Draffin, and Barby had gone along the track to Johnson's Well and farther round the Lake to begin operations.

The afternoon of that day found Bony interested in Ray Gillen's motor-cycle. He had gone to the large machinery shed which housed the station trucks, machine parts and materials, in order to repair a girth buckle. The motor-cycle was completely covered by a tarpaulin, and the dust on the tarpaulin supported statements that the machine hadn't been used or moved after Gillen vanished.

Bony lifted the hem of the covering. It was obviously a powerful machine, and had been maintained in good order. Bony felt the tyres, and they were firm. About the cap of the petrol tank was a wide ring of dust darker than the rest, and Bony smelled petrol. He removed the cap, and found the tank was full to capacity. The tank had been filled some time during the past two weeks, and Bony was confident it must have been done during the week before he arrived at Lake Otway.

He was sure that whoever had filled the tank and perhaps pumped air into the tyres had, like himself, not wholly removed the tarpaulin. When he dropped the hem of the covering, the dust remained heavy on the level surface. All evidence indicated that the machine had not been moved since its owner vanished fifteen months ago, and yet someone had prepared it for a journey.

Came the evening when he decided to take Witlow partially into his confidence, and it happened that the wiry little stockman himself provided the opportunity. Dinner was over and the Swede had started a game of banker in the sitting-room of the quarters, and Bony joined Witlow, who was darning a pair of socks on the veranda. Witlow lost interest in the socks and stood to wipe perspiration from his face.

'What about taking a swim in the Lake?'

'In two feet of water?' objected Bony.

'Two feet six inches,' corrected Witlow. 'Do a bit of wading. Splash about a bit. Cooler, anyway. Rux up the birds, too. Something to do.'

'Yes, all right,' Bony assented. 'As you say, it will be something to do.'

Witlow changed into a pair of shorts and Bony put on a pair of drill trousers needing to be washed, and in bare feet they descended the bluff steps to the 'shore' of the Lake and stepped into the water.

It was distinctly warm, and the bottom was hard beneath an inch of sludge. They had to proceed fifty-odd yards before the water reached their knees, and another fifty yards before it rose to their hips. The water was loaded with algae, faintly green in colour, and it was impossible to see far below the surface.

Witlow gave his humorous chuckle and splashed Bony, and Detective-Inspector Bonaparte shed thirty years. Gasping, yelling like small boys, they showered each other, and the nearer birds indignantly skidded away.

They continued wading towards the centre of the Lake, the depth not increasing. Before them the water was almost constantly disturbed by fish, the surface being ribbed, being sliced by dorsal fins, often for a moment broken by the broad back of a large codfish.

Like flotsam pushed aside by the bow of a ship, the ducks and moorhens swam to either side of the two men, and closed in again behind them. The great fleets of pelicans appeared to be motionless and yet kept their distance, and so with the swans and the cormorants. Some fifty-odd gulls accompanied the men as though expecting to be fed with crusts.

The water came no higher, and its temperature remained cloyingly warm. The air above it was hot to the skin, and the westering sun was the blinding centre of a vast flame. When Bony looked back and estimated they had waded a mile from shore, the distant homestead was aureoled in conformity with the crimson face of the bluff.

'A fortnight of this weather will finish the Lake for another twenty years,' predicted Witlow, and knelt on the bottom so that his head looked like the head on Salome's platter. 'A hundred and four again today in the pepper-tree shade. It'll go twenty degrees higher before this summer busts.'

Bony knelt and managed to sit back on his heels, when the water tickled his chin. He could not forbear smiling at Witlow, who said:

'We shoulda brought a couple of chairs out here. Funny, ain't it, being so far from land. Crook if the tide came in quick like it does up Broome way. Hey, stop your tickling, Jock. Oh, you will, will you? All right, brother.'

He appeared to lunge forward, his face going under. He came up, crouching, and lifted from Lake Otway a codfish weighing in the vicinity of twelve pounds, the fingers of one hand up under the gills. Then he lowered the fish into the water, played with it for a moment, and let it go.

'D'you know what, Bony, that feller just came and leaned against me. I put me hand on him, and he still leaned. Just like a lovin' cat.'

'There's one leaning against me right now,' Bony said. 'I'll try to grab him.'

He failed, and then, being abruptly serious, he said:

'Don't much like the idea of groping after fish. Might catch hold of Gillen's skeleton.'

'Yair, could do,' Witlow agreed, also sobered by the thought. 'He must be around somewhere, all the meat eaten off him by the yabbies.'

'Were you here when it happened?'

'No.'

'Good swimmer, too, wasn't he?' Bony nonchalantly asked.

'So they say,' answered Witlow. 'Still, fresh water ain't like the sea, and although it was a clear night the wind had been blowing all day and the currents out here musta been still running. Some say that after a windy day the currents run round and round like a whirlpool, and having swum out about this far Gillen woulda been in the centre and couldn' swim out again to the land. Anyway, he must be around somewhere. Crook if you or me happened to kick him up.'

Bony stood, feeling a chill down his back which had nothing to do with the prevailing temperature. He recalled a man much older than Witlow who had kicked up a corpse in a lake surrounding a place known as Venom House, and it was not an experience he wished to share. Witlow chuckled.

'Ain't likely,' he said. 'No more likely than winning Tatts. Big lake this, and a body's mighty small. Look at those birds.' A vast fleet of pelicans had drawn closer. 'An idea! Let's shift 'em. Both of us yell and splash at the same time.'

The effect of their efforts was explosive. The entire surface of the great Lake was thrashed with spurts of spray as the fleets of pelicans, the swans and wild geese, the countless ducks and the cormorants all skidded over the water to take to the air, the alarm passing from bird to bird with the speed of light.

'Look at 'em! Look at 'em!' shouted Witlow.

A chain of swans swung by, low above them, and the swans were bright red. The gulls fluttered as though nervous of being rammed; they were crimson and reminded Bony of Dampier

Bay and Broome where the widows were murdered. Crimson fire flashed from the plumage of whirring ducks, and the white markings of the pelicans grandly wheeling in great wedges looked to the men like splashes of blood.

'What d'you know about that?' yelled Witlow. 'The bleedin' Battle of Britain. What d'you . . .'

Abruptly he sat down, floundered, came up again spitting water.

'Strike me pink if a flamin' fish didn't charge through me legs,' he complained.

The birds gained height. The pelicans and the swans and the geese became armadas of heavy bombers, pounced upon, attacked by the meteor-swift ducks. The cormorants weaved as though completely bewildered, and the moorhens dived to the surface and huddled together as though in conference. And higher than the mighty bombers and the streaking fighters, the eagles spun their invisible webs beneath the scarlet sky.

Sudden and powerful pressure was applied to Bony's left leg, and he could feel the slimy body of the fish cannoning off him. It seemed, too, that all the fish had gone berserk, for his legs registered continued collisions, and the limpid surface of the lake was like a huge pot on the boil.

'That's worth wading out here for,' he said, and Witlow nodded agreement.

The sun went down behind distant trees whose ghostly shadows raced to them, passed them by, yet held them with threat of inevitable night. The water slowly became placid, and the fish quietened. The smaller ducks came tumbling down the airways to shoot long arrows of lilac spray as the water braked them. But the big birds remained aloft.

The two men began the journey to the shore, without haste, a little awed, for both were close to this spirit of Australia so impervious to Time and such finite matters as the birth and death of a lake. The distant bluff and the buildings upon its summit now were purpling, the shadows between the buildings like jet. The gulls flew on ahead, their colour now of gentian blue.

'What do you reckon about the blokes around here, Bony?' asked Witlow a trifle too casually.

'They aren't very pally,' Bony replied, easily.

'Can't nail 'em down. Must be the women what's upset 'em.'

'One would think most of them were old enough not to be upset by women.'

They plodded onward for a space in silence before Witlow said:

'You could be right, but the conditions ain't usual. I hitched to a drovin' outfit one time bringing cattle out of the Territory. Two men run the outfit, both of 'em older than either of us. Hard doers, too. Fight and booze artists. Been cobbers for twenty years. They thought only about cattle and grog and racehorses. And then an abo joined up, and he brought his gin with him. Young gal she was, and ugly as hell. Inside a week them two old bastards were in holts, and if I hadn't given the abo the wink to get going and take his gin with him, them two blokes would have murdered each other and the cattle would have scattered all over Australia. Day after the gin departed, they was back to usual. Beats me.'

'They say a man is apt to slip when he's seventy, or is it sixty?' Bony said, laughingly. 'There's certainly something eating the lads here at Lake Otway.'

'Sure thing, Bony. Remember the night you got asked to play cards with the women, and me and the Swede went with you to see there was no cheating. And then what? Ten minutes after we started playing, in comes Bob Lester, all friendly and interested, sniffle and all. After him comes Mac . . . you know, just dropped in to borrow the flat-iron or the fry-pan or something. Next comes Harry Carney, joking about being scared of being in the quarters all by himself. Me and the Swede was talkin' about 'em yestiddy. We never got close to them three, and somehow they stick together and yet snarl at the drop of a hat. Remember that brooch Ma Fowler was wearing that night?'

'Yes. An opal set in gold. Good stone, too.'

'Lester give her that,' Witlow went on. 'A hundred and twenty quid he paid for it.'

'What!' ejaculated Bony.

'A hundred and twenty. He told me. The emerald ring she's wearing she got from MacLennon, and Lester give Joan the wristlet watch she had on that night. He paid forty-five guineas for it. Then the ear-rings and the thing she had in her hair

Carney give her. Cost him twenty pounds for that lot.'

'How the devil do you know who gave what and what was paid?' asked Bony.

'That's the screwy part of the set-up,' replied Witlow. 'You see, those mutts simply got to tell someone about it. Lester tells me about the brooch, and skites that when he's saved a few more hundred quid Ma Fowler will be taking a trip with him to Sydney, and he gives Joan the watch to back him up with Ma. Mac tells me about the ring he gave to Ma, but he don't know that Ma promised Lester the Sydney trip; he tells me Ma promised to go on a bender with him to Adelaide soon as he's got plenty of money to pay for the trip. Then Carney tells me about the present he gives to Joan, and says he's keeping sweet with the mother till he pays up for Joan on the lay-by. See? All just between 'em and me or the Swede, if you know what I mean. J'u know what?'

Bony asked.

'There's going to be crackers and volcanoes before long. You can see it hotting up. Them two women are schemers all right. Proper trollops. Take a mug's advice and go easy, Bony. Better spit at 'em than smile. Me and the Swede could see what they was up to, that night we played cards. Smiling all over you. Cooing at you, and giving me a glad eye now and then, just to work up those mutts to send in to the office for a big cheque for more jewellery or something. And I ain't so sure that Martyr ain't a mutt, too.'

'Martyr!'

'Yair. Joan has a sort of bracelet all made with opals. Could be worth anything.'

'But why d'you think Martyr gave it to her?'

''Cos none of the others told me or the Swede about that, and that bracelet is something to boast about, believe me.'

'Did they ever put it on you for a present?' Bony asked.

'No. But Joan put the hard word on the Swede for the loan of fifty quid, and Kurt told her he had to support six kids in Norway, pay alimony to a wife in Sydney and keep a woman up in Cairns. Them big birds is coming down. Let's watch.'

The pelicans came down in wide curves and spirals. The swans dropped in steeper descent. A pelican fleet turned to line ahead, followed the leader like black-and-white links of an everlasting chain. The leader skimmed water less than thirty feet from the two heads, and every succeeding bird touched water at the same spot, followed the same braking line, moved to the right or left of the leader to form a vast crescent, each ship with its yellow 'bowsprit' dipped in salute to the Lake. The ducks continued to dive and skate in foam to a cheeky halt at the men, then swam lazily about them as they proceeded to wade to the shore.

'Be interested in a little bet?' drawled Witlow.

'You name the odds,' suggested Bony.

'All right! Betcher there'll be a murder within five miles of this out-station before Easter. Four to one in favour.'

'Sporting enough,' agreed Bony. 'In for a pound.'

7

It Pays to be Dumb

HAVING GAINED FREEDOM of movement without arousing speculation, Bony rode one of the youngsters along the sandy track leading to Johnson's Well. From the Well the track flowed over uplands of belar, pine and mulga, for thirty miles to the eastern border of Porchester Station, on and on to pass by the homesteads of two settlers and so to the railway at the town of Ivanhoe. It was by this track that Gillen had come to the out-station of Lake Otway.

It could be conceded that there are better places for meditation than the back of a young horse on a very hot afternoon, but the heat gave the horse something to think about and, being entirely devoid of humidity, was not unpleasant for the rider.

So far Bony could make nothing square in this mystery of Ray Gillen and his vanished treasury.

All that had emerged for the intuitive Bony was that those men and women who were at the out-station when Gillen announced his intention of going for a swim now waited with anxiety for Lake Otway to die. What did they expect, or dread, or hope from the death of the Lake? Did they foresee that, when the sun had sucked up all the water, the skeleton of Ray Gillen would prove he had not died from accidental drowning and thus start a murder investigation? Were that so, then five men and two women were associated in the murder, and this would seem exceedingly unlikely. Did they hope that, when Lake Otway dried out, the missing money would be exposed, and was it for this reason that every man and both women had continued in their employment here?

They were united by two bonds: their anxiety concerning the coming death of the Lake, and their front to everyone not present when Gillen went swimming for the last time. In all else, each of them was opposed to all the others.

Having reached this stage of his investigation, he was not dissatisfied with his progress, and again decided all he need do was to wait, when the people concerned would inevitably reveal exactly what did happen to Ray Gillen and his twelve thousand pounds.

At Johnson's Well he dismounted and neck-roped the horse to a shady cabbage tree. The well was situated on the bank of a creek some two hundred yards from the sandbar which prevented water running from the Lake when the level there was nineteen feet.

The hut was built with pine logs and had an iron roof. There was no glass in the one window, and the door required new hinges. Near the hut was the well, spanned by the windmill, and flanked by large iron tanks from which water could be discharged into lines of troughing for the stock. There was an engine shed and a supply of oil to work the auxiliary pump when the wind failed. Beyond the well were the horse yards, and an apparently abandoned reservoir tank stood in isolation between these yards and the engine shed.

A familiar scene for Bony: composed of sand and drowsing box trees, grey creek banks and flats, summer heat and flies, and, in winter, icy winds sweeping over the low dunes to keep the air heavy with gritty particles. A mere living place for men willing to put up with utter absence of comfort in order to earn a cheque.

Evidence of the work done by MacLennon and Lester was plain. The mill had been greased and the reservoir tanks were full, but the ball-cocks had been chocked with wood to prevent water running into the troughs. The oil engine had been serviced and run. There was, too, evidence that George Barby had been here with his utility.

The interior of the hut hadn't been touched. The floor was of packed rubble from termite nests. The long table was flanked by the usual forms. There was a bench under the glass-less window, and white ash still lay heaped on the open hearth. When Bony entered he disturbed a dozen rabbits, and they crowded into a corner and wished they had wings.

He had boiled water in his quart-pot and brewed tea, and was sipping the scalding liquid when he heard the rising hum of a motor engine, and was not at all surprized when Barby's brown utility heaved over the hard sandbar and came along the creek bank, empty water tins rattling, and three dogs barking at the tethered horse.

Barby stopped at the tanks, waved to Bony and proceeded to fill his tins. The dogs came across to make friends and then lie in the hut shadow with Bony. One of the rabbits charged out through the doorway, and the dogs simply were not interested. They accepted rabbits with the boredom with which they tolerated their stick-fast fleas.

Barby eventually came over to squat and load a pipe.

'What are you doing here?' he asked. 'Layin' off?'

'Toughening a youngster,' replied Bony. 'Where are you camped?'

'Couple of miles round the Lake. There's millions of rabbits coming to water, and I'm gonna fence a strip of coast and trap 'em.'

The cook was no longer a cook. He wore a grubby grey flannel vest, old and patched tweed trousers and rubber-soled sand-shoes which once could have been white. The sun already had sizzled his face and bare arms, had puckered his hazel eyes and stiffened his brown hair.

'If I had a farthing for every rabbit around this Lake,' he said with slow emphasis, 'I'd claim to own half Australia. Heard over the air once that there's five million rabbits in Australia. Well, all but ten of 'em is drinkin' at Lake Otway.'

'All but ten million?'

'All but ten. Eight, nine, ten. Those ten is down at Canberra laughing at the scientists. You think that mysotis any good to bump off all the rabbits in Australia?'

'Myxomatosis!' corrected Bony. 'No. It's partially effective,

I think, on small farms and along rivers where the mosquitoes are busy.'

'The rabbit'll beat the scientists, don't you reckon?' Barby persisted.

'The rabbits will beat any germ, any man, any thing,' Bony said with conviction. 'What the people in the cities and towns cannot grasp is the immensity of this land mass called Australia, and another thing they cannot grasp is that the Australian rabbit has been fighting droughts, sun, eagles and foxes, poison baits and George Barbys for a hundred years, and is still winning.'

'Too right they have,' Barby agreed, earnestly. 'Nothing's going to stop 'em. Why, the young does when they're six weeks old begin to litter fives and sevens every six weeks after. They're the greatest breeding machines that ever was. Let 'em multiply, I says.'

'They do eat feed and drink water needful for stock,' Bony mildly countered.

'So what?' Barby asked. 'They ain't doin' no real harm to Australia. The rabbit is the poor man's food and always has been. If the scientists do knock them out, which they won't, and if the squatters do rear twice as many sheep, will the price of mutton be any lower? Will the cost of blankets and clothes be any cheaper? Or the price of tobacco and booze come down any? No hope. But the squatters and the farmers will be able to buy more motorcars and machinery to rust away in the paddocks, 'cos they're too damn lazy to put 'em under cover, and they'll pay a bit more in taxes to let the blasted politicians have more world tours and get higher pensions when the people heaves 'em out into the cold, cold snow. And that's all the scientists are being paid to bump off the rabbits for.'

'Don't worry,' soothed Bony. 'Brer Rabbit will last for ever. How are you to clean them up here?'

'Drop-netted fences. Stop 'em getting to the water. Or stop 'em makin' back from water. Water they must have. And feed they must have. Wish Red could turn up. Me and him can skin five thousand a day. He's a champ. And five thousand a day for five years wouldn't be missed round Lake Otway. How are you gettin' on with the gals at the out-station?'

The unexpected question momentarily rocked Bony.

'Pleasantly enough,' he replied disarmingly.

'Bit stuck up with you?'

The indirect reference to his birth was not missed. As it was not intended to hurt, Bony took firm hold of the cue and played the stroke.

'Perhaps they think I'm dumb. A caste earning good money. Be nice to him, and he'll be persuaded to send down to the city for expensive presents.'

'That's about it, Bony. They never tried it on me, but there's them they have. Chisellers, they are. Been here too long. But blokes like me and you can see through them. You hear about the feller who was drowned in this Lake?'

'Yes. Red mentioned him at dinner one day.'

'Name of Gillen, Ray Gillen. Went swimming in the Lake one night and stayed put. So they say. Me and Red has other thinks about that. I was trapping at the time, but living at the men's quarters. Things were getting sort of tense, if you know what I mean.'

'Oh! How, tense?'

Barby had let his pipe get cold, and he picked up an ember from Bony's fire, balanced it on the bowl and drew noisily.

'It's a sort of history,' he said. 'Beginning from when them women came out from Broken Hill. Everything was smooth as pie then and they certainly made a difference. The young 'un could ride; Martyr used to take her out to look at the Lake and things.

'Then, accordin' to Red, there was a sort of bust-up. Red added a sum and probably got the wrong answers, but Martyr suddenly stopped taking the girl out riding. Seems that the mother complained she was left to do all the work, but it could be she was jealous at the daughter getting off with Martyr.

'Anyhow, after that it got sort of quiet, right up to the time Gillen came. He came from Ivanhoe way, and he had to push his bike the last half-mile to this place 'cos it broke down. He had tucker with him, so he camped a day or two right here and tried to fix the bike. When he couldn't, he walked to the out-station with the part that wanted fixing, and it happened all the blokes were out. So he stayed there till Martyr came home, and Martyr repaired the part and gave him a job the next morning.

'From then on things hotted up at the out-station. Both the women fell for Gillen, and he was supposed to be after the girl. Then there was a fight between him and MacLennon, and although Mac's done some ring work, Gillen beat him. He'd take the girl out on his bike. Then he'd take the mother for a ride, and they didn't know which of 'em he was after. He almost came to bashing Carney who camped with him and, being of about the same age, they sort of stuck together. Lester said something cross-eyed, and Gillen floored Lester, and apologized next morning. The women got into holts over nothing, so they said, but under it was Gillen. Then one night we all goes to bed, and he decides to go swimming, and that was the last anyone seen of him.'

'Any trouble that day?' Bony asked.

'No. Been no trouble for a week. The night he went for a swim we was all playing poker in the quarters.'

'Money?'

'No. Matches.'

'Gillen had a suitcase,' Barby went on. 'It was a flash case, too. He kept the key on a cord with a gold locket round his neck. And one day Red was sittin' on Carney's bed yarning to Gillen, and Gillen wanted a change of undies, and takes off the cord to open the case. And after he took 'em out he had to kneel on the lid to lock the case, it was that full.

'The day after Gillen was missed, Martyr got me and Lester to look see while he goes through the case to find out who Gillen's relations are. I didn't know then what Red saw about Gillen kneeling on the lid, not when Martyr opened the case. The case wasn't full at all. It was less than three parts full. It's only after Red and me talked it over that we wonder what happened to the inside of that case from the time Red seen Gillen open it to the time I seen Martyr open it. It wasn't as though Gillen's few things on the bed table made up for it. They didn't.'

Opportunity favoured Bony.

'You say Gillen always kept the case locked. And the key on a cord round his neck. How did Martyr open it?'

'How? Why, he just pushed the catches aside. Cripes, Bony! You're all there. I never thought of that angle. That case wasn't locked when Martyr opened it.'

'Martyr didn't have the key and the locket on the cord?'

'Not that I remember. No, he couldn't of had. Gillen had the cord round his neck. He never took it off, that I do know as well as Red.'

'And you think someone took something from that case?' Bony prompted.

Barby nodded, slowly, significantly.

'Yair, Bony. Money was took from that case.'

'Money!'

'A lot of money. I'll tell you why I'm sure it was money. Seven or eight days before Gillen got drowned, I was along the shore one night looking at me traps. There was a moon, good enough for me to work without a light, and I'm coming back from the end of me trapline . . . I was workin' a hundred spring traps . . . when I heard voices, and I just had time to slip behind a tree.

'I seen it was Harry Carney with young Joan Fowler. They wasn't walkin' arm-in-arm. Just walkin' polite. Joan says, calm as you like: "I'm not marrying on a few hundred pounds, Harry." And Harry says: "Well, the four hundred odd I've got saved up would give us a good start." She says: "That's what you think. It wouldn't go far these days. When I marry you you'll have to be rich. And you know what to do."

'Harry says: "Now look, Joan, I couldn't do that, even though the money musta been stolen, and he wouldn't dare to make a song and dance about it being stolen from him." Well, that's what I hear 'em say before they got too far away. I waited by that tree and presently they comes back, still arguing about a lot of money someone's stolen and what could be stolen in turn. Joan says: "Aren't I worth it, Harry? Think of the wonderful times we'd have. You know I love you." Harry still says he couldn't do it, whatever she wanted him to do about stealing stolen money. And she was still kidding him on when they got out of my hearing.'

'And you think Carney knew there was a lot of money in Gillen's suitcase?' Bony pressed, nonchalance well acted.

'Yes. I didn't know what to think at the time, but I thunk it out since.'

'But Joan didn't marry Carney, so Carney couldn't have taken money from Gillen's case.'

'That's so, Bony. But Carney knew the money was in the

case, and he told Joan about it. I'll bet he looked inside the case that morning he woke up and found Gillen hadn't come back. He could have taken the money then and planted it somewhere. Or someone could have beaten him to it. If it was the money missin' what sunk the tide in Gillen's case, then someone's got it and whosoever is still at the out-station, 'cos not a man left the place since Gillen was drowned.'

Bony looked dumb, frowning perplexedly at the cook-trapper.

'I don't get it,' he admitted. 'If anyone took a lot of cash from Gillen's case, then why didn't he go on a bender? If Carney took it why didn't he run off with Joan?'

'That beats me, too, Bony. But I'm as sure as we're sittin' here that Carney and Joan knew about a lot of money in Gillen's case, so much money that it must have been stolen. P'raps, when Carney wouldn't lift it, Joan got someone else to do it, and that someone double-crossed her. There's double-crossing all round, if you ask me. They're all like hungry dogs watchin' each other to find out where the bone's buried. And nicely planted that bone is, I'll bet.'

'You may be right,' conceded Bony, feigning admiration of Barby's perspicacity.

'I'm right enough,' Barby averred. 'And you and me could do a deal. You keep your eyes and ears open. Tip me off about what goes on over there. We might find that planted dough, and then we go fifty-fifty. We can easily face out in my ute, and nothing could be said by nobuddy.'

8

Effervescence

ANOTHER WEEK WAS devoured by the year, and nothing happened save that the two aborigines were sent with sheep to Sandy Well and Lester returned to his chores as rouse-about. Now the thermometer registered above the century every day, and the Lake began to look grey and tired.

One still morning an audience waited within the deep

shade cast by the pepper tree, an audience comprising nine dogs chained to roughly-made kennels and a young woman dressed in white. Her hair held the sheen of bronze, and her eyes . . . well, dogs, of course, are colour-blind.

Bony came riding a grey horse, and the girl laughed because the horse trotted. Only once had she seen a horse trotting with a rider up, and that at a Ceremonial Parade in Adelaide. When a hundred yards past the audience, Bony turned and rode back at a canter, and now the girl could but admire the action of the horse and the seat of the rider. They passed for the third time, at a gallop, the red dust springing away from the grey-tipped arrow.

Horse and rider returned again to pose for the audience, the horse standing like a statue. The pose was broken abruptly when Bony fell off the horse and lay on the ground with a foot trapped within a stirrup-iron. The girl became genuinely concerned. The horse remained a statue. Bony twisted his leg in an effort to free the foot, and the girl cried:

'Can I help? Shall I grab his bridle?'

Bony tugged at a thong, and the stirrup-leather parted from the saddle. He stood, smiling at the astonished girl. He returned the stirrup-leather to the saddle, dropped the reins, walked a little way from the horse and pretended to shade his eyes to admire a view. The horse flicked a fly away with an ear-waggle. Bony went back to him, leaned against a shoulder. Nothing happened. He shifted position and leaned hard against the animal's rump, the toe of one foot resting negligently on the instep of the other. He lit a cigarette, blew smoke elegantly skyward, and asked:

'D'you think he'll do?'

Joan Fowler's eyes shone, and Bony was immensely pleased with himself, for he was experiencing one of the lesser triumphs so vitally necessary to the maintenance of the pride which sustained him in the eternal war of the two races fighting for his soul. The feeling of triumph passed, leaving him refreshed.

'He's not one of the youngsters, is he?' Joan doubted.

'He was a youngster three weeks ago. Too soft yet for real work. Like to ride him sometime?'

'I really would.'

'You shall. But no prolonged gallops.' He smiled and she

forgot he was twice her age. 'D'you think I've earned my morning smoko?'

'Of course. It must be time.'

'Then we will return this gentleman.'

He removed the saddle, slipped the bridle, and the horse found a sandy patch and went down for a roll.

With the girl beside him, he ignored the horse and walked to the yards, in through the gateway. The horse got up, undecided what to do until he heard Bony's whistle, whereupon he trotted into the yard and bunted Bony's back.

'I expect he wants his piece of cake.' Bony produced a handful of crumbly cake from a pocket and, leaving the horse in the yard, they proceeded to the annexe for smoko.

'And Mother's been thinking you men got down on her cake extra well these last two weeks,' Joan remarked.

'You have no idea how your mother's cake has been appreciated,' he said gravely, although his eyes twinkled.

'I do now.'

'Keep the secret of training horses . . . until I've trained my last horse at Lake Otway.'

Mrs Fowler was sitting at the men's table, her dark eyes smouldering, her lips smiling. Joan poured tea for Bony and herself, saying:

'The Boss ought to be here soon. He left at seven, so Mr Martyr told me.'

'You're not dressed up like that because the Boss is coming,' her mother stated vehemently. 'What's the idea?'

The veneer of sophistication returned to the girl. Her eyes were masked by insolence, and deliberately she baited:

'Don't be jealous, Mother.'

Faintly perturbed by the expressions on their faces, Bony suavely intervened.

'No quarrelling, now. It's much too hot. A hundred and nine in the shade.'

'You keep out of it,' snapped the elder woman. 'And while I'm on the subject, let me tell you this. You're only a temporary hand here, and I won't have you and Joan slinking away and scheming.'

'Mother! That's enough.'

'That's what you think. I'm not blind nor soft.'

'You are both, my dear parent,' sneered the girl.

'And you're nothing but a brainless clot. You've proved that time and again. You're so full of yourself you think no one can see round corners.' The woman swung back to Bony. 'And you're a bigger fool than you look if you believe anything she tells you.'

The girl attempted to speak, was shouted down. Bony calmly sipped his tea, hoping to learn more about women.

'She's only using you up,' Mrs Fowler continued, her voice raised and dark eyes blazing. The storm of anger suddenly increased so that her voice shook and syllables slipped. 'She's got you in and she'll bilk you, like she's bilked others. Young and luscious, eh? The itch of any man. But I'm warning you she's more poisonous than a bottle of strychnine. Don't you . . .'

'Why don't you go and jump in the bloody lake?' asked the 'young and luscious'. 'You've had your day and can't take it, that's what's wrong with you. Shut up!'

'You . . .' Mrs Fowler fought for control enough to scream the words. 'You fool, you couldn't even seduce a sailor.'

'Enough, my lady mother. Let's have a cup of tea in peace.'

'And I'm not soft,' went on the older woman. 'Neither is MacLennon. He'll stop your slimy tricks. And if you think we don't know about your little schemes you're mistaken. You won't get away with any more. You won't . . .'

Joan snatched up the milk jug and dashed its contents against her mother's face. She held the jug behind her shoulder to throw that, and Bony hastily removed it from her hand before she could resist. The mother gasped and wiped her eyes with the hem of her apron, and the girl turned on Bony.

'Get out and leave me to calm her down.'

There is a time for masculine discretion, and this was it. Bony filled his cup, took another slice of cake, and retreated. The door slammed shut behind him, and he sat on a case and continued his smoko. He had been there less than a minute when Lester appeared, and the watery eyes lit with momentary interest and the sniffle was almost an explosion.

'You chucked out?' he inquired.

'Requested to leave,' corrected Bony.

'Are they at it again?'

'They are at it again, Bob. Pause awhile to give them time

to cool. Otherwise you may have the tea-pot thrown at you.'

Lester sniffled and squatted on his spurred heels with admirable dexterity.

'Seems they got things on their minds.'

'What things?'

'Oh, this and that. Could be each of 'em thinks the other's got something they haven't.' He stood up, 'Well, I'm goin' to chance my luck. I'm dry.'

'Then take my cup in. You might need ammunition.'

Bony chuckled and brought another sniffle, and he left a little hurriedly as Lester made for the door. Glancing back he saw Lester on the step, his hand turning the door-knob, and a look of cunning concentration on his face.

Other than himself and Lester, no other man was in for lunch. The cold meal was set out for them. Neither woman appeared. Throughout, Lester was thoughtful and spoke but little. Witlow came in from his day's job just before the afternoon smoko, and when they were strolling to the annexe, the Swede joined them. The tea and cake were on the table, but the women were still absent.

Lester was still moody, and Witlow was about to chaff him when the irrepressible Swede cut in with:

'How hot today, Bony? 'Undred and eighty?'

'A hundred and nine.'

'Looks like March won't see no water in the Lake,' observed Witlow.

'Pelicans leave soon, I bet,' Helstrom laughed at an undisclosed joke. 'P'raps tonight. I bet level pound no pelicans here tomorrer.'

'Keep it,' said Witlow.

'You not sports, eh?' He stood up and tapped his chest. 'Me, I real Australia. All yous New Australians. Not sports. You too soon in Australia for to be sports.'

'You were, I suppose, born at Snake Gully,' smiled Bony.

'Me! Na! I been in country forty-one year. I real Australia. How long you been in Australia?'

'Forty-one minutes.'

Helstrom roared with laughter.

'Ya! I tink now why you spik like Bob Menzies. What place you born, eh? London?'

'Yorkshire.'

'Yorkshire!' The Swede indulged in ponderous thinking. Then he grinned and shouted: 'Ya! You got any brass?'

The Swede certainly was one big bright boy, and only Lester failed to appreciate him.

'What's wrong with Sniffler?' Witlow asked when they were on the veranda, and the rouseabout had saddled a horse and gone for the cows.

'Maybe he's worried because the women had a fight at morning smoko,' Bony surmised. 'They ordered me out, and I told him to give them time, but he would go in and probably had his ears blistered.'

'Ah,' murmured Witlow, smiling satisfaction. 'Working out, eh! Well, you're going to have it all on your own. Me and Kurt's shiftin' camp in the morning.'

'Oh! Where?'

'Takin' ewes into the River. Fifty miles is too far to be handy when it happens.'

'When what happens?' Bony asked quickly.

'You took me up on the murder bet.'

'So I did,' Bony drawled. 'I shall be collecting four pounds from you.'

'I'll bet a pound you won't.'

'Now we're becoming involved. Straighten out.'

'All right. I lay you four to one there'll be a murder hereabouts before shearing starts. And I lay you a level pound I win that bet. Sort of a bet behind a bet.'

'It's as well for me that you are leaving. When were you told?'

'This morning at orders.'

'Sorry about the move?'

'No. Much better on all counts at the River.'

'You will have your cobber with you.'

'Yair. Me and Swede get along. You're gonna be lonely.'

Bony agreed and crossed to the yards, and had been there only a few minutes when a new and large American car brought the large Mr Wallace, owner of Porchester Station. Wallace must have noticed the dust being kicked up by the horse Bony was handling, for he walked stiffly from the car and hauled himself up to sit on the top rail. There Bony joined him.

'How's things?' asked Wallace.

'Could wish for a spell of cooler weather,' replied Bony. 'The grey there has turned out well. You want him, Martyr said.'

'Yes. Always liked that gelding. My second daughter's coming home next week. Good enough for her?'

'Should be. Leave him with me for another week.'

'All right.' The large man eyed Bony sideways. 'How's the other business coming along?'

'My interest is being sustained,' replied Bony, and Wallace was astonished to see no smile accompanying the statement. 'How long will the Lake last?'

'A week at most if the heat continues. Important?'

'It seems to be,' admitted Bony. 'Don't ask me why. You could perhaps work out a small problem. I understand that Kurt Helstrom and Witlow are leaving here tomorrow for the River. You knew of that?'

'I knew that forty-four hundred ewes would begin the move to the river country in the morning.'

'Not that the Swede and Witlow would be taking them?'

'No. I leave the hands at this end of the run to Martyr. Martyr is a good man. The best overseer I've had. Always believed in loading responsibility on those who can take it. What's the problem?'

'I am presented with what is probably a coincidence, and if coincidence or not, I must determine,' Bony said. 'It's a subject I must ask earnestly that you treat confidentially. When Witlow and the Swede leave Lake Otway tomorrow, there will remain the seven people who were here when Gillen vanished.'

Wallace produced a pipe and filled it, taking his time, and lighting up before he spoke again.

'Coincidence.'

'But . . . When did MacLennon and Carney and Lester last go down south on a spell?'

'I must think that one out. The book-keeper will know.'

'Inform me later. I know that these men haven't taken a holiday since before Gillen vanished fifteen months ago. That applies also to Mrs Fowler and her daughter. What about Martyr? Doesn't he take annual leave?'

'Yes, of course . . . What the hell is on your mind? He was due for leave after Christmas, and the Christmas before last he didn't take it; said he couldn't afford to as his mother had to undergo an expensive course of treatment for something or other and he was her sole support.'

'Very well. We can leave Barby out as he has a reputation for saving money. You have six people, all here when Gillen vanished. Not one has left even for a holiday. Normally everyone would insist on taking a break from this isolated place. Martyr, you say, selected the Swede and Witlow to move the ewes. Could you invent a reasonable excuse for suggesting to Martyr that Witlow be retained and one of the others sent?'

'Yes. What's the point?'

'I want to know if Martyr purposely selected those two men, or if he offered the move to one or two of the older hands and they refused it. Living conditions at your homestead by the River would be superior to those ruling here, don't you think?'

'Yes, of course. Regular mail. Close to Menindee. Fair amount of traffic passing through. I see what's on your mind. Any man here ought naturally to want to change to the river homestead.'

'That is so. When anyone doesn't react naturally, I am elated,' Bony said, beaming at Wallace.

9

A New Experience

BONY RELAXED ON the edge of the bluff. It was almost totally dark, and he had watched the night extinguish the furnace colours on and above Lake Otway. The Swede would have lost his bet had anyone taken his odds on the pelicans leaving, for last seen by Bony they were gathered in close-packed mobs like crowds about road accidents. Now it was night and the only sounds to reach Bony were the conversations of water-birds and the radio in the house behind him, for the men were at dinner in the annexe.

All the people who were at Lake Otway when Gillen

vanished were here this night, save Barby in his camp across the Lake. The only addition to this community was himself, a supposedly itinerant horse-breaker. Before Wallace had left to return to the big homestead he had made clear the selection of Witlow and Helstrom to take the ewes to the River, having ascertained from Martyr that the overseer had offered the change to MacLennon and Carney as they had been working much longer at the out-station. Both these men preferred to remain, the former because he did not like change and the latter because the pubs at Menindee couldn't be far enough away.

This cleared up a minor point concerning Martyr, a point which would have had to be considered had the overseer not given those two old hands the opportunity of change, but it stressed the significance of the fact that those two men had remained constantly at Lake Otway, and were determined to stay on.

Wallace had agreed to probe Red Draffin and the point to be raised was the suitcase key, the key to the true fate of Ray Gillen. Draffin had said Gillen always kept his case locked and the key on a cord round his neck. This was supported by Barby. When Martyr, with Barby and Lester, examined the contents of the case the day after Gillen was missing, it was not locked and the key wasn't seen by Barby. Draffin said the case was so full that its owner had to kneel on the lid to close it; Barby said the case was but little more than half full when they had listed the contents.

That neither Draffin nor Barby had informed the police or even Wallace of their suspicion that something of value had been removed from the case was quite in character, for neither had closely associated with Gillen and, like the average bushman, they would not want to be drawn into a police inquiry. In none of the police reports was there mention by Gillen's room-mate, Carney, of the key worn by the missing man ... or mention of it by anyone else.

Bony was considering the implications behind the progress of his own investigation when there was a light step behind him and he turned to see a dark figure approaching.

'I was hoping you were still here, Bony,' Joan Fowler softly said. 'I want to talk to you. You won't mind?'

'No. I won't be lonely now.'

Together they sat on the edge of the low bluff where steps had been cut. The girl said:

'We must talk quietly, 'cos voices carry, and I've sneaked out. I saw you here before it got dark. You know, I've been thinking a lot about you. D'you think I was very terrible to sling that milk at Mother?'

'Red Draffin, I think, would have suggested even sterner measures. It would seem that your mother can be very difficult.'

'She won't believe I've grown up and all that. You don't really like me, do you?'

'Not to like you would be plain silly,' was his cautious response.

'I don't mean just that way. I mean, well, you know how I mean, don't you?'

'How do you mean?'

'Now you are being difficult. Just imagine. When I go to meet a man, he wants to kiss me to show how much he likes me.'

'Ah! But you see, Joan, I am married, and you are Temptation.'

She restrained her laughter . . . and moved close to him.

'Being married's got nothing to do with it, Bony,' she whispered. 'You men! You aren't all the same, no matter what Mother says. Some want to smother me; others, you for instance, have to be told. Kiss me, please.'

The danger of being seduced had never been previously encountered by Inspector Bonaparte, but one kiss would be both pleasant and ungallant to refuse.

'That was nice,' Joan sighed, resting her head against his shoulder. 'Do it again. You like me now, don't you?'

'Yes. You are very desirable, but I . . . I am unseducible.'

'I haven't really tried yet.'

'What else can I do for you?' hastily Bony asked.

'Would you do anything for me, Bony?'

'Bar throwing milk at your mother.'

'Are you still my friend?'

'I have, I hope, proved that.'

'I must go back.' She swung her body round to confront him, and he could see the starlight in her eyes. 'Mother will wake up to me if I don't. Will you do something for me . . . please?'

'Tell me.'

'What would you think about a man who promised to marry you and, because he came into money, wanted to get out of it?'

'If you are the lady, the man needs the attention of a psychiatrist.'

'A what?'

'Mental doctor.'

'Oh! Yes, he does ... Now you've made me admit I'm the girl. Well, so I am. Mind you, I wouldn't marry him now, but I'm not letting him get away with it.' Joan moved closer. 'Pity you are pure, Bony, but I'm glad you'll help me. I've no one I could trust to see that I get a fair deal.'

'I shall make sure that you get a fair deal,' he told her.

The girl fell silent, and Bony waited.

'A long time ago,' she resumed, 'Harry Carney made love to me. You know how it goes in a place like this. No amusements, nothing much to do, nowhere to go. He promised to marry me, and I believed him. Then he went cold and called it off, and I made him tell me why. He said it would be silly to marry on a station hand's wages, and that's all he'd have until his uncle died and left him a pile. When I said we could wait, he said his uncle might live for another thirty years even with a sick heart.'

Joan fell silent again, possibly expecting Bony to jump in with indignant sympathy. Instead, he asked:

'How long ago was that?'

'Just a year. And lately I've been wondering about Harry. He's moody and restless, and I think his uncle died. I think Harry's come into his money, and I'm worried he'll sneak off and leave me cold. That's why I want you to help me.'

'How?'

'Just by watching him. You know, without him knowing. Just tell me when he starts packing up ready to go.'

'But he couldn't go without you seeing him put his things into the Boss's car or Barby's utility.'

'He could get away all right, Bony. There's Ray Gillen's motor-bike still over in the shed. Harry's good with a motorbike. We took it out one afternoon when Mr Martyr and the other men were away at the lamb-marking. We went for miles on it.'

'The lamb-marking? Last May?'

'Yes.'

'Only that time?'

'Yes.'

'But everyone would hear him start the machine. You would, too.'

'It would be too late then. Harry would be on it and off.'

Bony did not trouble to point out that before Carney, on the stolen machine, could arrive at Menindee to the south, Ivanhoe to the east, or Wilcannia to the north, the telephone could cripple the plan. Nor did he state the fact that Carney was intelligent enough to devise a far more subtle plan. Nevertheless, the motor-cycle in the shed had been prepared for the road.

'He'd persuade George Barby to give him a lift from here, Joan.'

'No, he wouldn't,' she argued. 'I know, because he's already got the bike filled with petrol. I watched him. It was the day before you came here, and he was supposed to be out riding. I happened to see him sneak into the shed, and ran over and looked through a crack in the wall. He was filling the petrol tank. I saw him unscrew things and clean them. Then he pumped the tyres and put the sheet back, and tossed sand on it to make it look dusty like it was.'

'H'm! Could be serious,' conceded Bony.

'I know what I'm talking about.'

'You have given that impression. You want me to watch him?'

'Please, Bony.' Her hands pressed his shoulders. 'Will you . . . for me?'

'Very well. Now off you go, and you don't have "to be kind to me".'

Flippantly, she tilted his chin, jumped to her feet and ran, and he waited a minute before strolling to the men's quarters. Someone cut the dynamo motor, and the result relieved the mind and freed the ears to register other noises. Within the house a radio gave music. From the Lake the birds called. In the men's sitting-room Carney was writing a letter and Lester was reading a paper through spectacles perched on the end of his long nose.

Instead of entering, Bony sat on the broken chair and rolled a cigarette. He wondered what lay behind Joan Fowler's inducement to persuade him to watch Carney, discarding the absurd story of the rich uncle, and having to accept the fact of the motor-cycle being prepared for a getaway by Carney.

A figure loomed into the light from the living-room, and when the man mounted the veranda Bony saw MacLennon. MacLennon obviously noticed the glow of Bony's cigarette, for he paced the veranda and sat with his back against a rail post.

'Took a chance and cut off that damn engine five minutes ahead of time,' he said. 'Gets on my nerves nights like this. I hate it when the wind don't blow.'

'Could be no wind for weeks at this time of year,' Bony pointed out. 'Getting near the end of the sheep lift?'

'Yes. Passed the last flock to go to the fellers at Sandy Well. Martyr's given us a day off tomorrow. Crook on the sheep, too, movin' them in this weather. Not so good, either, on the horses, I suppose.'

'That's so.' Bony tossed the cigarette butt over the rail and began to roll another. 'The Swede and Witlow are lucky to be going to the River.'

'They can have it,' MacLennon said, a trifle sharply. 'Too much spit and polish there. Martyr's easy compared with the Boss. You see the end of your contract in sight yet?'

'About three weeks.'

'You'll see the Lake dry out.'

'Looks like it,' agreed Bony. 'Pelicans seem to be preparing to go for good. Water down under two feet by the marker this evening.'

'It'll go quick at the end.' MacLennon struck a match and held it against his pipe, and the illumination revealed his square face and powerful shoulders. The black moustache, always trimmed and snipped short, partially balanced the broken nose. He spoke with the slow deliberation of the punch-drunk, and often put a punch into his speech to emphasize a point important only to himself. 'Find Ray Gillen when she dries out, I expect.'

'The feller who was drowned some time ago?' queried Bony.

'Yes. Went swimming one night. Musta got cramp. Ruddy fool.'

'How so?'

'Been a hot day. Hot night, too. First heat of the summer, it was. He always tore into the water at the run. Worst thing out for getting cramp. Owed me forty quid, too.'

'Bad luck,' sympathized Bony.

'Yes. I won it at cards. Not all at once; over a coupler weeks. He said he would pay up some time. Offered to give me a gold locket as security. Me, I'm a fool. I told him I'd wait for the cash. Ought to have took the locket. He always had it on a cord round his neck. Musta wore it when he went swimming.'

'Then it will be with his skeleton. Close by it, anyway, if the cord hasn't rotted by this time.'

'That's what I've been working out,' MacLennon said, keeping his voice low. 'I was thinkin' you might do me a favour if you happen to find Gillen.'

'How?'

'There's no knowing where the skeleton will be now. Could be anywhere on the Lake floor. Good place to exercise young horses . . . on the Lake when she's dried out. If you happened to find the skeleton, would you nab the locket for me? It's mine actually.'

'Yes, all right.'

'Good for you. And keep it dark from the others. Suspicious lot of . . .'

Above the noise of the radio reverberated an explosion, the house walls making the sound deep and hollow.

'Gun!' exclaimed MacLennon and heaved up from the veranda. Bony vaulted the railing and ran to the house, raced up the wide steps to its front veranda. There were lights seemingly in all the front rooms. The door behind the fly-netted door was closed.

Bony was conscious of the others behind him.

'Gun, wasn't it?' queried Carney.

'Sounded much like it,' Bony said and pulled open the fly-door. He was about to knock on the inner door when somewhere within the house a woman screamed hysterically. Then came Joan Fowler's voice raised to shouting pitch.

'Stop it, you damn fool!'

There was a bumping sound and the noise of pounding feet. Bony knocked heavily on the door, and behind him MacLennon rumbled:

'Get in! Get in! Sounds like a rumpus.'

Bony thrust the door inwards to bang against the wall of a short passage. At the end of the passage stood Martyr in his pyjamas. In his right hand he held a 12-bore shotgun.

Somewhere along a cross-passage Mrs Fowler was hysterically crying, and they distinctly heard the face-slap momentarily stopping the hysteria. A door slammed, cutting the whimper threatening renewal of the screaming.

'What happened?' asked Bony, and was relieved of tension when the overseer leaned the weapon into a wall corner and advanced to them.

'An accident,' he said, evenly. 'Nothing for anyone else to worry about, when Joan can pacify Mrs Fowler. I was cleaning my gun when it went off. Didn't know it was loaded, and I could have sworn it wasn't.'

'Funny time to be cleaning a gun,' growled MacLennon. 'Do any damage?'

'No, I don't think so. The charge went into the floor. Everything is all right.'

The air was heavy with burned powder. From a distant room Mrs Fowler could be heard sobbing.

'It's quite all right, Mac. You can get back to the quarter,' Martyr told them.

He was unusually pale, but his voice was steady. He stood with his hand on the door preparatory to closing it. Lester sniffled and that touch of normalcy killed unreality. And unreality was buried when Martyr said:

'Good night!' and closed the door.

10

An Unsolvable Mystery

DUE TO HIS lifelong habit of waking at dawn Bony witnessed the first throe of the coming death of Lake Otway.

On waking he proceeded, as usual, to roll a cigarette and while doing so recalled how the pelicans had congregated in great crowds on the previous evening. He had slept on the top of his bedclothes, and it was now as hot as when he had fallen alseep.

On bare feet, he passed out to the veranda and sauntered to its end overlooking the Lake.

The birds still congregated. He counted eleven masses of them in a rough line along the lake's centre, each mass looking like an island on which now and then someone waved a white flag. The flag was the white of under-wings when a bird raised itself and flapped its wings as a cat will stretch to limber up.

The sky slowly acknowledged the threat of the sun. The surface of the Lake caught and held the same threat, and when the edge of the sun lifted above the trees behind Johnson's Well, the first bird took off.

The unit detached itself from a mass, flapped its great wings, paddled strongly and began to lift. When air-borne, the bird took the long upward slant as though bored with flying. Another bird followed, a third, and so on to form a chain being drawn up to the burnished sky by a magnetic sun. The same routine was followed by the other congregations of pelicans, until there were eleven long black chains over Lake Otway, each link rhythmically waving its white flag.

When a thousand feet above the water, the leader of each chain rested upon outspread pinions, and those following gained position each side of the leader and also rested. Thus a fleet was formed, which proceeded to gain further height, every 'ship' of each 'fleet' alternately winging and resting in perfect unison.

The chains having been wound up and the fleets formed, the sky was ribbed and curved with black-and-white ships, each with its golden prow. Like ten thousand Argosies, they sailed before the sun, fleet above fleet, in circles great and small as though the commanders waited for sailing orders.

Presently the fleets grandly departed, one following the other, the units of every fleet in line abreast, sailing away to the north till the sky absorbed them. Fifteen, twenty years hence that same sky would produce similar fleets of Argosies to sail down the air-ways and harbour on Lake Otway reborn.

'They must have felt the bottom with their paddlers,' Carney said, and Bony turned to the young man whose face defied sunburn and whose large brown eyes seemed always to be laughing.

'What's the tally?'

'Be a wild guess. Ten thousand, perhaps,' Bony essayed.

'Could be more. The swans took off some time in the night, looks like.'

'One foot ten inches of water left, by the marker. Bottom of the Lake flat all over?'

'Like a billiard table excepting at Johnson's Well end,' replied Carney. 'There the creek extends into the Lake for about a hundred yards. They call it the Channel. Water will stay there for some time because the Channel is twenty feet deep, and the sandbar keeps it from running out. The banks being steep and slippery, it's a trap for stock, which is why the flocks watering at the Lake had to be shifted.'

'You will be sorry to see the Lake die,' Bony said, and Carney nodded and his eyes, Bony fancied, became wistful.

'When she's full, Lake Otway makes this place worth while,' Carney said. 'I'd like to own this country and have Lake Otway full all the time. How would it be with a light yacht to sail on windy days and an aquaplane to pep things up?'

'You forgot the fishing-boat,' Bony added, to make the picture complete.

There was a boat here, brought out soon after the Lake filled. We used her for fishing and bathing from. Then we got an east wind, a real beaut, and it raised short up-and-down waves that pounded the boat to splinters. We ought to have had sense enough to pull it well up the shore-line. Now there's barely enough water to float a loan.'

Carney was propounding a 'brilliant idea' to keep Lake Otway permanently filled when Lester appeared to give his first sniffle for the day. On being told that the pelicans had departed, he said no respectable bird could be expected to 'lollop around on a plate of soup,' and Bony noted that Carney's moment of loquacity ended.

Who had cooked the breakfast this morning was not evident. The dishes were placed on the table for the men to help themselves. Nothing was said of the gun incident, and afterwards the men loafed about the quarters and Bony went for his horses, including the grey. At the morning smoko gong everyone crossed to the annexe, and again neither woman appeared.

'Wonder how George's getting on with the rabbits?'

Carney said, obviously to lighten the general mood. He was supported by Lester.

'Ought to be doing pretty well. I never seen so many rabbits around this Lake before, and nowhere else for that matter. You can go anywhere and holler and choke the burrows with 'em. It's goin' to be the fun of Cork when the water dries out and leaves only the Channel. There'll be so many rabbits drinking at the Channel, old George and his dogs and cats and galah will all be buried under the rush.'

The sniffle was almost a snort, and Bony said:

'As I am going to spend the night with him, I'd better warn him.'

'You oughta give up breaking and go in with George,' suggested MacLennon. 'Make more money in one night at the rabbits than any of us would make in a month. Wouldn't mind giving it a go meself.'

'Not me,' supplemented Lester.

MacLennon scowled into his tea-cup.

'We'll all go in with George,' he said. 'Harry'll want to, I bet. And Martyr won't be left out. The women could come along, too, and cook for the gang.'

'Suits me,' drawled Carney. 'But no guns.'

'No guns,' agreed MacLennon. 'Guns go off on their own account late at night. George wouldn't like that. Make him nervous.'

Lester cackled, and raised a laugh.

'A grain or two of strychnine if you like, but no guns.'

'Seems to be a joker in the wood heap,' Bony mildly surmised, and MacLennon glowered.

'Yes. Bloody funny. We'll cut the talk and stick to rabbits. If we're all going, we'd better get Red Draffin out to lend a hand. Told me he could skin five hundred an hour when he got his hand in.'

'Bit over the fence, that one,' objected Carney, and Lester argued.

'You want to see Red in action. If he can't do five hundred, I'll back him to do four ninety-nine. Tried myself out once and got up to ninety-nine.'

Bony left them discussing famous tallies and went back to his work, and an hour later was surprised to see Joan sitting on the top rail of the yard watching him. Today she wore navy-blue slacks and a blue blouse, and blue wasn't her colour. When he joined her to roll a cigarette, he asked:

'How is your mother? Recovering from the fright she received?'

'She's all right now. Sleeping it off. Shock, you know. The sound inside the house was terrific.'

'It must have been. Who did fire the gun?'

He looked at her, watching her mouth frame the words:

'Who fired the gun? Why, it went off when Mr Martyr was cleaning it. The idiot! Messing about with a gun at that time of night.'

'Where was he cleaning the weapon?'

'It sounded in his room. Said it went into the floor. When are you going to let me ride the grey?'

'Tomorrow afternoon. Suit you?'

'Yes. I'll be able to manage him?'

'I shall be riding with you.'

He swung his legs over the rail to sit facing across the open space and the light-drenched Lake beyond.

'All the pelicans left this morning,' he said. 'The swans went during the night.'

Joan swung herself round to face the Lake. The house was then slightly to their left. Bony said:

'I have been wondering what caused the hole in the house roof above your bedroom.'

Receiving no support at this turn of the conversation, he looked directly at her. Her face was expressionless, and her eyes were green, like bottle glass.

'You don't believe Mr Martyr when he says the gun went off while he was cleaning it?'

'The hole in the roof wasn't there yesterday. Martyr could have been cleaning the gun in your room, and the gun could have been pointed at the ceiling when it was discharged. The iron roof is quite low to the ceiling, and the Number One shot did not expand to make a cullender of the roof, as you can see.'

'You were outside looking through the window?'

'I wouldn't dare.'

'Then how did you know where my room is?'

'Because the slacks you are now wearing, and which are so nicely pressed, were lying over the window sill. What did happen last night?'

'I told you. You wouldn't know, anyway.'

Joan climbed down to the ground, where she turned and looked at him, head up, an insolent smile curling her mouth. He smiled at her, and her mind was held by his eyes, deep blue and unwinking, and they grew in size and threatened to read her secrets. Then he released her.

'You'll ride the grey tomorrow?'

'Of course. And we're still friends?'

'If you will permit.'

'Then say nothing about the hole in the roof.'

'As your friend, why should I?'

She laughed, turned to make for the house, said over her shoulder:

'Thanks. You're improving. See you sometime.'

Bony found Martyr working in the office after lunch, which was served by Mrs. Fowler, now her usual self. Tentatively, he told the overseer his intention of spending the night with George Barby; the alert pale-blue eyes in the weathered face were speculative until their owner nodded agreement.

'How are you travelling . . . per horse?' Martyr asked, and when told Bony would walk, he offered the use of the station utility. With assumed shyness, Bony declined the offer, saying he would prefer the walkabout, and Martyr nodded understanding of the urge which often cannot be resisted by aborigines.

Thus, in the late afternoon, Bony went down to the Lake and followed the short line round to Johnson's Well. The clear burning heat dried his throat, and the glare of the water seared his eyes, so that he turned a tap in one of the reservoir tanks and drank the comparatively cool water. Thereafter, he sat in the shadow cast by the tank and fell to making another of the everlasting cigarettes.

Relaxed, he went over again the reactions of those whom he had told of this trip to Barby's camp for the night, and arrived at the same conclusion – that no one of the men appeared abnormally interested, or betrayed even a hint of pleasure at being relieved of his presence. The short conversation with MacLennon the previous evening during which emerged the ex-fighter's interest in the gold locket worn by Gillen occupied him for five minutes.

Then he wandered about this Johnson's Well, hauling himself up to look down into the water filling the reservoir tanks. Wire netting was stretched across the tank-tops to prevent birds drowning and fouling the water. He removed the boards covering the well, and would have gone down the ladder fixed to the shaft had he been certain about the air below. The discarded tank attracted him. It was smaller than those in service, and he guessed its capacity to be three thousand gallons. Its circular wall appeared to be in fair condition, but then it is always the floor of an iron tank which first rusts out.

Without difficulty, he hauled himself up to look inside, and received one of the great surprises of his life.

It was filled almost to the brim with the carcasses of cormorants. They had been there so long that the sun had mummified them, and there was no evil smell other than the faint musty odour. How many? There must have been several thousand birds that had piled into this tank to die.

11

The Trapper's Camp

BONY FOLLOWED THE creek bank to the dune blocking it at the shore of Lake Otway, and on his walking over the ramparts of blown sand the Lake in all its mystic colour stretched before him.

The continuance of the creek beyond the sandbar and out into the bed of the Lake was plain enough, the Channel being forty yards wide and said to be one hundred yards in length.

The buildings of the out-station were blobs of red-and-white atop the red bluff, and much nearer, on the opposite shore, was the white patch of Barby's tent set up in the meagre shade cast by an ancient gum. Everywhere in the shallows extending from both sides of the Channel, ducks were busy, but the herons and other waders fished with such marked indifference as to cause Bony to wonder why they wetted their feet. Flocks of moorhens ran about the dry flats, and galahs sped under the arches of the metallic sky as though to prove to earth-bound men that nothing created by nature has straight lines.

On the wide strip of dry land between Barby's camp and the dwindling water of the Lake, Barby had erected a flimsy fence of wire netting in the form of a very broad V, the point of the V thrust into the wall of a high netted trap about ten by ten feet. Now the netting was lifted off the ground and hooked to the top of the posts, mere sticks hammered into the earth. The rabbits would soon begin their evening journey, from burrows and every inch of shade on the sand dunes and the uplands beyond, to drink at the Lake, and after dark they would be out on the flats in countless numbers. And then Barby would lower the netting, making sure of a wide selvedge on the ground, and in their efforts to return to their burrows and feeding grounds, the rabbits would drive to the point of the V, pass through a hole at the point and so into the great trap.

Barby was cooking at his fire. Close by the tent was the utility, the tailboard being Barby's table, and a wooden case his chair. Under the vehicle were his three dogs, who on sighting Bony ran excitedly to meet him. The black-and-white cats came from somewhere to add their welcome, and the galah, who had perched on the tent ridge-pole, became so flurried it forgot to fly and slid down the canvas to 'flop' on the ground and emit screams of injured dignity.

'Day, there!' Barby shouted long before Bony drew near. 'Seen you coming, so I've boiled the billy. How's things?'

There being nothing to shout unnecessarily, Bony deferred an acknowledgement of welcome until he stood watching the trapper laying a bread dough in a bed of hot white ash.

'Thought I would put in a night with you,' he said. 'How is the fur coming?'

'Staying the night! Good on you. Fur's coming in like a ruddy flood. Two thousand pelts last night. Could have got five thousand if Red had been with me. You sighted him at all?'

'No.'

'Give us a bit of a hand in the morning?' Barby asked, anxiously. 'Tea's in the billy. Sugar and pannikins on the table.'

'I could lend a hand for a couple of hours,' Bony said.

He filled a pannikin, added a morsel of sugar. The dogs subsided. The cats daintily rubbed against his legs. The galah waddled over the ground on its clumsy pigeon-toed feet, tumbled on its back and looked up at him with hard bright eyes.

Barby covered his bread dough with the ash, plus an addition of tiny red coals, careful to spread the heat. Because his face had been darkened by the sun his eyes were inconspicuous, but they were no less quick, no less alert.

'Goin' to be even hotter tomorrow, by the look of that sun,' he remarked. 'Hope it keeps up. Hotter she is the thirstier the rabbits.'

'Did you see the birds go?'

Barby nodded.

'You don't see a sight like that down in the stinking cities,' he said with emphasis. 'Or that.'

Bony followed the direction of his out-flung hand and witnessed a rabbit unhesitantly come running from the dunes, its normal timidity vanquished by the onslaught of thirst. It followed a straight line to the truck, stopped in its shadow for a moment, moved on and over the foreleg of one of the dogs. The dog lifted its upper lip in a sneer of disdain and continued panting. It did snap at a fly. The rabbit ran on to the flat, seeking the water it must drink or perish.

'Why in hell I own dogs I don't know. Fat lot of use, ain't they? Well, I'll knock up a stew for dinner.'

'What can I do?' asked Bony.

'Do! Nothing, just yabber. How's things on the other shore?'

'Everyone is a little moody.'

'Watchin' each other, eh?'

'And the Lake.'

The galah determinedly tried to detach tabs from Bony's riding boots . . . until a flock of galahs whirled overhead, when it twisted its head to look up at them. Barby shouted to Bony to 'grab him', but Bony was too late. The bird took wing and sped upward to join his kind.

'Now we'll see something, I hope,' Barby predicted. 'But one day he won't be coming home.'

Barby's bird joined the flock, which proceeded to put on a turn of aerobatics for the benefit of the stranger. The stranger could not be distinguished, for its performance was as flawless. They flew about the camp tree, shrieking at each other and the watchers, and presently there emerged from the general cacophony a sepulchral voice:

'Ole fool! Ole fool!'

The same line was repeated several times, when the entire flock converged upon one member. The movement revealed the Ishmael, who, uttering a wild shriek, headed for the camp and arrived fast, to land on the cabin of the truck, skate off to fly in a semicircle to Barby's feet, skid to the ground and then swear with extraordinary fluency.

'That'll be enough out of you for one day, my lad,' Barby said, severely. 'Where you got that Australian language, I don't know. You never got it off me.'

Taking up the bird, he locked it in the netted cage and, continuing to glare like the parent of an unruly child at a party, proceeded with the preparation of the stew, saying not a word until a vast shadow moved over the camp. The caged bird muttered threats, but not at the passing eagle.

'Plenty of them about,' Barby told Bony. 'Ordinary times they keep to their own beats. Now they're here in thousands.' The eagle, golden of neck and wedge-shaped tail, swung out over the flats, and the trapper carried forward the argument whether eagles do greater good by killing rabbits than the reputed destruction of young lambs.

The sun went down when the stew-pot was simmering, and Barby lifted from the ashes the feather-light loaf of baking-powder bread. The rabbits were leaving the uplands, crossing the dunes like drops of dark-brown ink, passing the camp on either side, taking no fright of the dogs and the cats, and unnoticed by them. An uncountable host was beginning to converge on Lake Otway.

Barby fed his dogs on kangaroo meat and filled their drinking dish. The cats received smaller pieces of meat, and he put a handful of sunflower seeds on a plate with damper crusts and passed it to the galah. The galah promptly emptied his dinner on the floor of the cage and threw the plate away.

Night appeared . . . stepping from the Lake. Night draped its garments over the surrounding flats, pulled down the red dunes, reached for the slopes of the uplands. The pestiferous flies went home, and the men ate at peace with themselves and with this land which never has been and never will be the servant of man.

Barby went to work on one of the wings of the fence-V, and Bony attended to the other, lowering the netting, making sure the selvedge lay flat. The hole at the apex of the V inside the great trap was examined by Barby. The stars were hazy, and the silence was hot.

Afterwards they squatted on their heels either side the camp fire, where Barby drew at his pipe and Bony smoked cigarettes and betrayed his maternal ancestry by constantly pushing together burning ends of wood.

'I looked into that discarded tank at Johnson's,' he said. 'D'you happen to know what is in it?'

'I do. Shags. Millions of 'em.'

'How do you think they died there?' prompted Bony.

'Don't know. No one does. It happened after the flood came down, when the Lake was pretty full, so there was miles of water for them birds to swim in.'

'How soon after the floods arrived?' pressed Bony as Barby appeared to be thinking on something quite different.

'How soon? It must be about three months after the Lake filled up that I was at Johnson's, and the shags were in that tank then and ponging high.'

'Although the tank was discarded, it could have held rainwater?'

'That tank wasn't discarded,' Barby said. 'She was took there from the River to make an extra reservoir tank, but before the stand could be built the flood was coming, and nothing was done about it.

'Martyr and me and Ray Gillen was deciding about them shags one night. Just after the flood entered Lake Otway it rained more'n five inches in one hit. That was the first rain for fifteen months, and the last decent rain we've had. It must have put five inches into that tank.

'The shags, of course, are flying round. You know how they get wet and sit on fence posts and up in dead trees, droopin' their wings to dry off. There's water then in a bit of lake down the creek, too, and those birds was flying from one to the other. One of 'em sits on the tank to dry off, and he could've seen a tadpole in the rainwater and went down for it. Then there isn't flying-room for him to get up, and while he's flopping round, a cobber sees him and went in, too. Then the others followed on to get trapped in the same way.'

'It could have been like that,' Bony conceded, doubtfully.

'Never heard of a better argument to explain it.'

One of the cats jumped to Barby's shoulder, settled there and purred like an engine. Foxes barked near and distant. The faint sound of rabbits passing by could be heard when the men were silent. Presently Bony asked:

'D'you think Martyr is careless with guns?'

'Didn't ought to be,' replied Barby. 'Been handling guns since he was three and a bit. Why?'

'It appears he was cleaning a shot-gun late last night and it was accidentally discharged.'

'What time last night?'

'About twenty minutes after ten.' Bony related the details. 'There's an inaccuracy in Martyr's story. He said that the shot went downwards in the floor, but there's a hole in the roof which wasn't there in the afternoon. The situation of the hole in the roof is peculiar. When the gun was discharged it must have been pointing upwards at the ceiling in Joan Fowler's room.'

'Perhaps the gun was pointing at someone, and someone else knocked the barrel up just in time.'

'If it was like that, George, then the two women and Martyr are hanging well together. There was no one else in the house.'

'And Ma yelled and screamed, and had to be slapped down.'

'We could hear the slaps.' Bony repeated the talk in the men's dining-room at the morning smoko, adding: 'It appeared to me that Lester, for preference, thought one of the women might be in the kitchen and wanted her to know that the tale of the accidental gun discharge wasn't believed.'

'Could be that way,' agreed Barby. 'Lester's more cunning than the other two added up. Born and reared in this part of the country. Like me, the other two wasn't. Where d'you reckon Harry Carney could have planted the money he took from Gillen's case?'

The tacked-on question astonished Bony, but gave him an instrument to use in the near future.

'Under that load of cormorants,' he replied, chuckling.

'By heck, you may be right at that, Bony. Fancy burrowing

down among all them birds to plant a wad of money. Imagine the pong while he was doing it. Well, we'd better think of some shut-eye, for we're due to rise at sparrow-chirp. I can lend you a wool-pack to lie on.'

Bony slept on the wool-pack until an hour before dawn, when Barby beat him to the bell by announcing breakfast consisting of kangaroo steak, damper bread and coffee.

Soon after the meal, the Lake began drawing Night down from the upland ridges, and Bony sat with Barby on a low dune providing a clear view of the latter's trapping plan. A little wind came from the north, and even after all the sunless hours it was hot.

The rabbits that had been drinking when the netted arms of the V were lowered had, of course, found their way back to the shore dunes blocked by the fence, and taking the course of least opposition had arrived at the point of the V. Inside the trap all the ground was covered with them, and at each corner living rodents sought freedom by standing on a heap of suffocated rabbits.

Outside the trap the animals were vainly seeking passage to the dunes and, like drops of water trickling from a tap, so they found the hole at the V point and trickled into the trap. Farther out on the flats rabbits ran as though from an enemy, to be slewed by the fence arms and so to run towards the point.

'You'll see something in a minute,' forecast Barby.

Bony saw the eagles, winging low along the verge of the water. One angled and skimmed the ground, then shot upward: another came on and delayed its swoop until opposite the camp. The rabbit leaped but failed to evade the talons. It screamed when a thousand feet high. Now all along the shore the eagles worked, their wings spanning six to seven feet and as rigid as the wings of a plane until they needed power for the lift. To and fro flew the eagles, and all the rabbits out in the open raced for the dunes and cover, and all the rabbits inside the tips of Barby's V raced dunewards, to arrive at the trap.

No eagle missed. Some snatched the victim without touching the ground with a claw; others paddled like the pelicans for a yard or two. Some dropped their catch from a height and swooped to retake the victim before its muscular death-twitching ceased.

'They do that every morning for me,' Barby said 'Good workers, eh?'

'Saves you a lot of rushing about,' agreed Bony.

'They don't last, though. One rabbit to each eagle and the supply of eagles soon runs short. We'd better get out there and stop them rabbits breakin' back.'

The dogs went with them as they circled eventually to walk inwards between the extremities of the fence. The men shouted and hoo-hoo-ed as though droving sheep, but the dogs were blasé and useless.

The rabbits crowded into the V point. Many hundreds did manage to break back, and when Barby cursed a bored dog, the animal deigned to grab one and break its neck.

Bony assisted Barby with the skinning, raising his hourly tally to eighty-three. At the end of the third hour, thanks to Barby, they completed this chore with the night's catch of close on two thousand rabbits. Barby was most appreciative when Bony left him slipping the skins over U-shaped wires to be stuck upright in the sand to dry.

12

A Night Out

WITHIN BONY'S PHILOSOPHY of crime investigation was the conviction that if the criminal became static immediately following the unlawful act he had every chance of escaping retribution, and when this, rarely, happened in an investigation he was conducting, he countered by prodding the suspect to activity.

On his way back to the out-station, he decided on a little prodding, and the opportunity came at the afternoon smoko when again he met the two women, Lester, MacLennon and Carney, the men having returned early.

'Have a good time?' asked Carney, and MacLennon raised his dark brows and seemed to await the answer with unusual interest.

'Yes. Quite a change from horses,' Bony replied. 'Helped

George to trap and skin just under two thousand. He netted the same number the night before.'

'My! What a big pie,' exclaimed Mrs Fowler, again vivaciously dark and off-setting her daughter's vivid colouring.

'You wouldn't believe how thick they are a bit away from here,' Lester put in. He sniffled before adding: 'This side of Johnson's Well they're thicker than sheep being druve to the yards. And foxes!'

Bony, munching cake, was conscious of Joan's eyes, but resisted looking at the girl in order to outwit the watchful Carney. MacLennon grumbled:

'And after what they said the myxotossis would do, too.'

'If the floods and droughts can't wipe out the rabbits, the mosquitoes and germs haven't a chance,' Lester said. 'Look, four years ago there wasn't a rabbit anywhere within a hundred and fifty miles of this place, and I hadn't seen a rabbit for eighteen months. Then one day I saw a rabbit on a sandy ridge, and a month afterwards rabbits were burrowin' and breedin' like mad. Them city fellers can't even imagine how big Australia is. They think the rest of Australia is another suburb or something.'

'And they won't believe rabbits drink water, either,' declared Mrs Fowler. 'When I said they did, I was called a liar.'

'Caw!' Lester sniffled twice. 'Rabbits'll drink water and they'll climb trees and gnaw off the suckers and then go down to eat the leaves. When there an't no grass, they'll scratch up the roots. And wild ducks will lay their eggs a mile from water, and lay 'em up in trees, too. Won't they, Bony?'

'Yes. And cormorants will fill a three-thousand-gallon water tank up to the brim.'

'Ah! You had a look in there?' asked Joan, and Bony now met her eyes and, while nodding assent, decided they were blue.

'George was telling me how it must have happened,' he said. 'But what I don't understand is why the topmost birds died there when they could have waddled to the side, stepped up to the rim and flown away.'

'But . . .' Carney began and trailed, and impulsively Lester asked:

'How far down from the rim d'you reckon them birds is?'

'Three inches. Not more than six.'

The almost colourless eyes dwindled, then flashed examination of the others.

'Them birds was down eighteen inches when I seen 'em last.'

'When was that?'

'When? Year ago, could be. You tell George about that?'

'That the level of the birds was almost up to the rim? No.'

'I wonder what raised them,' murmured Joan, gazing steadily at Bony.

'Some chemical change which has gone on since Lester looked in the tank. The action of heat and the air and what not might have caused each carcass to expand a fraction.'

'Sounds likely,' supported MacLennon. 'I still can't believe the yarn how they got there.'

'Give us a better one, Mac,' urged Mrs Fowler.

He shook his head, grinned and lurched to his feet. 'I'm no good at inventing lies,' he said, and went out. There was silence for a space, broken by the girl.

'You sure, Bony, about the level of the birds?'

'Reasonably so, but I could be mistaken,' replied Bony. 'I merely pulled myself up to look over the rim just to see what was inside. A few inches down from the rim was the impression I received.'

'I expect the crows got at the carcasses and stirred them up,' Carney volunteered. 'Say, Bony, did you ever see the sun suck a dam dry?'

'Only once,' recalled Bony, aware of the effort to change the subject. 'It was one of those days when the sky is full of dusty-looking clouds that never pass under the sun to throw a shadow. I happened to be heading for a dam containing seven feet of water in a twelve-thousand yard excavation. It was 112 degrees in the shade, like today, and no wind. When I first saw it the water was being sucked up in a fine mist you could see through. The mist thickened to a light-brown rod, and then the rod densed and became dark brown, almost black, and suddenly it looked like a water spout upside down. At the top it formed a white cloud, and in two minutes the bottom of the rod was drawn up like those pelican chains we saw. When I reached the dam there wasn't enough moisture, let alone water, to bog a fly.'

'It doesn't often happen, then?' asked Mrs Fowler, keenly interested.

'So rarely that people who haven't seen it won't believe.'

'I believe it. I believe anything can happen in this country,' Mrs Fowler claimed, and Lester sniffled and told a story about fish coming up three thousand feet from an artesian bore. After that the 'party' dispersed, Bony satisfied with the initial effect of his prodding.

When darkness spread over the Lake he was sitting on his favourite dune well to the right of the bluff, and when the night was claiming the dunes, he caught sight of the figure stealing between the dunes and taking advantage of the low but sparse scrub trees. He thought it could be Lester.

It was dark when he moved. The light was on in the sitting-room, but the bedrooms were vacant. He drifted across to the house. There was a light in the annexe, but no one was there. On the side veranda the two women were listening to a radio play. He did not see Martyr.

In his room at the quarters, he stripped and put on sand-shoes. Because the light in the sitting-room could reveal him leaving, he slid over the sill of the bedroom window at the back, and drifted down to the Lake to follow the flats to Johnson's Well.

On arrival at Porchester Station, he was all Inspector in an efficient police department, but quickly assuming the role of horse-breaker, he travelled far from that lofty appointment towards the normal occupation and status of the half-caste. When he started out for Johnson's Well this early night on a mission of stealthy observation, he travelled beyond the half-caste to become all aborigine . . . save in the ability to assess the psychology and bushcraft of the white man.

The men at the out-station were expert in this bush of the Continent's interior where open space separated the flat plane of earth and sky. They knew their stars, and were familiar with the importance of sky-lines . . . the shape of things against the sky . . . so that movement in the normal dark of night was barely less curtailed than by day. Set against the aborigine standard the bushmanship of these station men was poor, but none the less to be respected.

Bony followed the flats all the way till barred by the sheen of water he knew to be the Channel. This he swam and continued towards Barby's camp before turning 'inland' and so reaching Johnson's Well.

Any tracks his sand-shoes might leave would be attributed to the trapper, and presently against a sky-line appeared the shapes of remembered trees, and then the short straight lines abhorred by Nature . . . the shape of the hut.

Here he waited to prospect with his ears. He could detect the scurry of rabbits, now and then the warning signal made by a rabbit thumping a hind foot on the ground, and a methodical thudding as of wood on iron. This last came from the direction of the discarded tank, and he guessed correctly it was made by a fork or shovel being used in emptying the tank of dead birds.

He had to bring the tank to a sky-line, and because the man at work was almost certainly being watched, the watcher or watchers had to be located.

He moved in a wide arc to cut the drift of the faint air-current bearing the musty odour of the dead cormorants, and then moved up-wind, progressing on hands and toes to reduce the danger of crossing an enemy's sky-line. Eventually he could see the level rim of the tank regularly broken when the worker tossed out carcasses.

In the air-line of the bird-odour lesser scents could not be registered. He moved to the right, and so was aware of the smell of a white man. The white man was lying against the steep bank of the creek, his head protruding above the bank, so that he had a clear night-view of the tank. He located the second white man positioned near the engine shed, and he also had a clear view.

Three men . . . one inside and two outside the tank . . . Lester, Carney, MacLennon. He doubted it was Lester among the carcasses because Lester hadn't been carrying a fork or shovel when last seen among the dune scrub at dusk.

He returned over his course to cut again the odour of the dead birds, and then warily proceeded up-wind to draw as close to the worker as possible in order to identify him on a skyline when he clambered out. And he had been in the selected position less than three minutes when he heard a suspicious sound . . . down-wind.

Bony brought his face close to the ground to obtain a sky-line to see what made this sound, the air current passing from him making his nose useless. The place was alive with rabbits. He saw the skulking shape of a fox moving swiftly and with enviable silence, and was sure the fox hadn't betrayed itself. Then he saw a shape without identifiable form, and knew it must be within a dozen feet of himself. It was advancing with extreme caution, slowly, silently, until its breathing identified it for Bony as a man. A fourth man.

Like an iguana Bony slid to one side, keeping that low-to-earth figure in view. It passed close by, continued towards the tank till it vanished in the complete darkness against it.

The fourth man? George Barby, or Richard Martyr?

The phrase 'It's gonna be good!' stirred in the well of his mind. He ordered memory to haul it to the surface while he lay inert, vision strained to register any movement against his sky-line. The implement being used to empty the tank was a garden fork. He could see the load of carcasses lifted above the tank rim, see the fork shaken, hear the handle bumped against the iron to free it. The man laboured diligently, yet it was some time before Bony heard the tines scrape over the iron floor as though searching for something.

'It's gonna be good!' Ah! An aborigine had said that nine years previously when he and Bony were about to witness, from the top of a tree, a brawl between two sections of a tribe.

A dark bulge grew atop the tank. Before it became recognizable a greater mass rose between it and Bony . . . that fourth man . . . When the fourth man moved slightly to the side as he advanced, the shape on the tank rim was like an enormous spider walking its web. On dropping to the ground he vanished and the sound of his landing came clearly.

Other sounds reached Bony, soft and sinister noises culminating in a sound like a snake being slammed against a tree branch by a kookaburra. A man shouted the one word 'You . . .' and then this same voice shouted 'By . . .' Again the snake was slammed against the branch, and the man said softly this time 'No!' as though saying it dreamily to himself.

There was a low scuffling in the black void against the tank. The man lying against the creek bed withdrew, rolling rubble down to the dry bed. Over by the hut, someone ploughed with devastating noise through the heap of tins and refuse. Then a shapeless thing loomed over Bony, and he slid to one side to avoid tripping the fourth man, who departed to the point from which he had first appeared. Thereafter there was nothing but the soft movements of the rabbits and the incessant conversation by the birds on the distant lake.

Bony retreated, covering a hundred yards without creating sound enough to upset the rabbits playing all about him. Now on his feet, he strode to the drafting yards, circled wide the horse yards and the hut and so arrived at the Lake on Barby's side of the Channel. He sprinted to the Channel, swam it with least noise possible, and began the four-mile journey to the out-station at a lope.

He had to be in bed before the men returned to the quarters, and first must ascertain who was about. That Mac and Carney had followed Lester, Bony was sure, but it could be that neither was aware of the other having trailed Lester. It could be that Lester had been trailing either Carney or MacLennon. Who the fourth man was, was a further item to accompany Bony as he ran silently over the flats.

The morning would reveal who had been bashed when he left the tank, either by his appearance or by his absence. Were his own absence from the quarters discovered, the guise of disinterested horse-breaker would be shot to pieces.

13

Lester is Confidential

THE HOUSE WAS without light, but the bulb still blazed in the sitting-room at the quarters. The dogs were quiet, yet the darkness might well conceal a watcher. Bony circled wide to reach his room via its back window, and found a watcher. She was within the deeper darkness of the machinery shed, and from her the exceedingly gentle wind conveyed to Bony her perfume. Joan Fowler's presence made him gamble with time. He spent five minutes seeking out other watchers, found none, and slid over the sill of his bedroom window.

Soundlessly he removed the sand-shoes and donned his pyjamas. That was easy. It was not easy to lay himself on his bed without making it complain, but he achieved it as the result of previous practice.

Silence was an empty stage upon which not even the calls of the water-birds intruded. Silence was an enemy defeated by inherited instincts and aboriginal training, but it triumphed over the white man. Bony heard the faint noise made by Carney, who entered the room next to his by the same ingress, the window.

Long, long minutes passed into limbo. Then the bed beyond the room occupied by Carney squeaked when MacLennon put his weight upon it.

As Lester occupied the bedroom on the far side of the sitting-room, Bony could not blame himself for failing to hear Lester's return.

More long minutes passed, when Carney moved and uttered a soft expletive. Bony heard him leave his room, then light steps on the veranda. He saw his dark figure looming in the oblong of the door-frame.

'Hey, Bony!' Carney called. 'You awake?'

'Wash that? What's marrer?' asked Bony.

'Got any aspirin? I've a rotten headache.'

'Aspirin! May be some in my case. Put the light on.'

Carney the bird digger? Carney making sure the horse-breaker hadn't been up to tricks?

Swinging his legs off the bed, Bony withdrew his case from under the bed and groped under its lid. He blinked at Carney. Carney was in night attire. His fair hair was ruffled. He looked undamaged.

'Don't know what I ate to bring it on,' he said. 'Thanks. I'll get some water. What time is it?'

'No idea,' Bony replied. 'Time for a smoke, anyway. Have you been out on a jag?'

'Been playing cards with the women. Only coffee to drink.'

The brown eyes were round and wary, and Bony purposefully fumbled with the cigarette paper and tobacco. They missed nothing, taking in the condition of Bony's bedding, his clothes, his boots. The canvas shoes they failed to see, for they were inside the case.

'Last man in left the light on, Bony. What time did you go to bed?'

'About half-past ten, I think. There was no one about, so I left it on.'

'Well, switch the ruddy light off and shut up,' shouted MacLennon.

'All right! All right!' Carney called, and winked at Bony.

He passed to the door, paused with his hand on the switch. Bony nodded and he switched off the light. Bony heard him pouring water from the bag suspended from the veranda roof. Then the sitting-room light was flicked off and Carney dropped on his bed as though intentionally making it complain.

The next morning he met Carney coming from the shower-house and inquired about the head.

'Good! Those tablets fixed it in five minutes,' replied Carney. 'Goin' to be a stinker of a day by the feel of the sun.'

'Seems likely.'

Bony showered and towelled. He heard MacLennon on the veranda when he was combing his straight black hair, and MacLennon was advising Lester to 'rise and shine', else he'd be late for breakfast. MacLennon needed to shave, but otherwise was tidy and clean, and he nodded to Bony when turning from Lester's room, saying:

'Bob must have gone off early after the horses.'

Carney carelessly agreed and joined Bony at the end of the veranda. They looked upon Lake Otway, an unruffled sheet of molten metal seemingly making afraid the gulls hesitant at the verge, and a cormorant perched on the marker. The level was thirteen inches. Carney said nothing. The breakfast call was given.

As usual, Mrs Fowler served the breakfast. Other than the 'good mornings' and the question and answer concerning Lester, conversation was at zero. Joan didn't appear. Carney was first to leave the table, and when Bony passed outside the annexe he found Carney gazing narrowly towards the horse yards.

Coming round the outside of the yards was Lester. He was on foot and carrying a bridle.

'Seems like Bob got tossed,' Carney remarked. 'Looks for trouble, Bob does. Won't put a saddle on the night horse, and that mare can't be trusted.'

Together they walked to the end of the buildings backed by the pepper trees and waited for Lester, who was dragging a foot. MacLennon joined them, and it was he who asked Lester, without evincing much concern, what had happened, Lester's jaw was dark with contusion. His head was awry. The right eye was bloodshot but not bruised. He sniffled and tried to jeer at himself.

'Heaved off,' he said. 'Treacherous bloody mare. Caught me bending as I was rounding up the mokes. The neck strap broke and she got free and cleared off on me.'

'Feelin' a bit sick, by the look of you,' MacLennon snapped, his lip lifted in a sneer of derision. 'Looks like you been fighting or something.'

Lester's eyes hardened and became small, like wet beach pebbles. He would have snarled a counter had not the quiet voice of the overseer slipped it aside.

'Go and lie down on your bunk, Bob,' Martyr ordered. 'I'll come later and practise on you. Mac, ride out to Sawyer's Dam after you bring in the workers. Bony won't mind you using his hack. Take a deck at the weaners. And get back as soon as you can. It's going to hot up properly, and there's no necessity for any of us to fry. By the way, you fellows, your light was on too late again last night.'

'Yair,' admitted Carney, who occasionally slurred his speech. 'Last up forgot.'

Martyr's pale-grey eyes hardened as Lester's had done, and he clipped:

'If it happens again, I remove all the bulbs. Some of the batteries are sick. The dynamo is sick. I'm sick of talking about it.'

They dispersed, Bony to saunter to the yards to await the return of MacLennon with the horses. He rolled a cigarette and watched the overseer walking to the office. Martyr suffered a slight limp. He came from the office carrying a medical kit and crossed to Lester's room. Ten minutes later he returned to the office, and five minutes after that Mrs Fowler crossed to the quarters carrying a breakfast tray.

At the morning smoko, Mrs Fowler had Bony to herself. She was wearing a coral-pink overall, which suited her, and she was evidently pleased with the situation.

'It's going to be unbearably hot today,' she said while filling the cups with strong tea. 'I do hate this heat.'

'Thermometer under the pepper trees says it's 108 degrees. It must be 208 degrees in your kitchen,' Bony guessed, and wasn't far off the mark.

'Must be . . . with bread baking. Your work must be exhausting.'

'Unfair to the horses. I'm knocking off at lunch for the day. Took a filly along to Johnson's Well to work off some steam. The Lake seems about finished, doesn't it?'

'Looks just yellow mud to me.'

'Who won last night?' Bony asked, and the woman's dark brows rose questioningly.

'But we didn't play last night. Joan was out somewhere till late. With you?'

'I've been here three weeks,' Bony said with assumed severity. 'Candidly, do I appear to you as a skirt chaser?'

'No – no, you don't, Bony.' Then she smiled. 'You could try yourself out some time. Keeps a man young . . . and a woman, too. Everyone's a bit slow here, you know. I'll bet you've had plenty of women chasing you before now. You can't make me believe you're not scientific.'

'Ah!' Bony breathed, and smiled his beaming smile. 'Once upon a time when I was young and bold I rode away with a squatter's daughter. The squatter and his men pursued us, soon caught up because my horse was carrying a double load. I'll take a cup of tea and a portion of cake over to Lester, if you don't mind.'

He stood and filled a pannikin.

'What happened when the men caught up with you?' demanded Mrs Fowler, and Bony wondered if she was being naïve.

'I dumped the lady upon a saltbush and rode on and on,' he said. 'And I never went back to that station. In fact, there are so many stations to which I cannot return that I have to think hard before asking for work at one.'

Smiling deep down into Mrs Fowler's warming eyes, he placed a piece of cake on his own plate and, with a cup of tea, wended his way to Lester, who was sitting on the broken arm-chair on the verandah. An expertly placed bandage was about the stockman's neck and much adhesive tape fixed lint to his jaw.

'How is the neck?' Bony asked.

'Not so bad. Bit stiff. Sort of ricked it when I hit the ground.'

'It mightn't have happened if you hadn't forgotten to wear your spurs.'

'You could be right,' Lester agreed. 'Tain't often I forget 'em. Musta been dopey. I woke up at dawn and couldn't get back to sleep, so I decided to go for the workers 'fore breakfast.'

'The first time you forgot them, too. The spurs, I mean.'

Lester glanced direct, then swerved away from the bright blue eyes. Quietly and with slow emphasis, he asked:

'You talkin' double?'

'For your sake, Bob.'

'How come?'

'If MacLennon tracked you when he went after the working horses, he mightn't find the place where the stable horse threw you this morning. Of course, if you thought to mess up the ground somewhere, and faked the horse's tracks where she was supposed to have bucked you off, it would substantiate your story.'

'Are you tellin' me I wasn't dumped this morning?' Lester asked.

'Yes. There is something going on here I don't understand. I'm here only to do a spot of breaking, and it's nothing to do with me, but I couldn't help seeing that neither Carney nor MacLennon believed you were dumped. After all, you've never done me a bad turn, and I'm only giving you a warning.'

There was another long silence, which Bony terminated.

'You see, Bob, it was like this. MacLennon could have noticed you forgot your spurs. You always wear spurs. You put them on when you dress in the morning as sure as you put on your trousers. There is something else, too. Someone has forked all the shags out of the tank at Johnson's Well. Was done last night. When you limped back this morning and told us your story, I could smell on you those dried birds. The smell wasn't strong, but you were to windward of MacLennon and Carney as well as me. It's no business of mine why you went to Johnson's Well and emptied that tank.'

The inevitable sniffle. A chuckle without humour.

'What else did you see at Johnson's?'

'Nothing.'

'Tracks you musta seen.'

'No. The rabbits wiped out your tracks.'

The possessive pronoun was not missed.

'You seen no other tracks?'

'As I said . . . the rabbits . . .'

'Yair, I heard.'

Lester pondered and Bony patiently waited. The veranda roof creaked under the torture of the sun. Beyond its shade the earth was polished by the sun, light red on the summit, dark red in the gullies of the miniature dunes kicked up by human feet all the way to the house on the far side of the open space. The shadows cast by the distant house, the out-buildings backed by the pepper trees, were black. White patches in one such shadow were the gasping hens.

'You know, Bony,' Lester drawled, 'there's something up between Ma Fowler and Mac and between Harry and Joan what's different to just playing ring-a-ring-a-roses. Right now those two women will be watching us, wondering what we're saying, wondering what we know and what we don't know. If I talk, you keep it to yourself?'

'Don't talk if you'd rather not,' urged Bony. 'As I've told you I'll be gone with my cheque in a couple of weeks. I mentioned those birds at Johnson's merely as a warning because I saw how suspicious Carney and Mac were this morning.'

'I know, and I'm not liking you less for it, Bony. It's because you're only casual, and because you got eyes, that I reckon you could do me another good turn. If y'would.'

'Of course.'

'Well, I got to start with them two women,' Lester proceeded and at once proved he could think straight. 'They came here, and mighty soon got everything changed over at the house and with the cooking and such. We could see they was on the make, but they was good sports and played around. You know how it is for a few blokes in a place like this.

'After Ray Gillen come here, things were stirred up a bit. Mac had been chasin' Ma Fowler and Harry had been after Joan when she was passed up by Martyr, who, I suppose, reckoned he'd have to be careful, or take the sack from Wallace. Ray was a good bloke in all ways. Them women played up to him, but he was too cunnin' to be properly caught. He'd take one and then the other out of an evening on his motor-bike. He'd tease 'em and make 'em wild, and kiss 'em when they wasn't expectin' him to, and all that. He was always crackin' jokes and bettin' he'd do anything better'n the next . . . and always winning, too.

'One day me and Ray was sent to patch up the yards at

Johnson's Well and we went there on his bike. We took our lunches as it was a long job. And that day Ray told me he was suspicious that someone had opened his suitcase and gone through his things.

'He swore he always kept his case locked, and that the locks weren't just ordinary and easy to pick. Always had the key with a gold locket on a string tied round his neck. I seen it there. Everyone did. Even when he went swimming he had that key and locket round his neck.

'We nutted out who could have got to his case when Ray was out in the paddocks. There was Carney who slept in the same room as him, and there was them two women always home when every man Jack of us would be out working. Any of us others could have tackled Ray's case, but would take a hell of a risk of being seen, going in or coming out of his room, by one of the women.

'I arst Ray what was in the case he was so particular about, and he said there was two hundred quid he had saved up. When I told him he ought to take it to the homestead to be locked in the book-keeper's safe, he said he could look after his own dough.

'Two nights after we pitched that day, he was drowned. Then Martyr got me and George Barby to be with him when he went through Ray's case to find out about his people or such. The case wasn't locked, that stonkered me, but I was more stonkered when there wasn't any money in it.

'I've never said anythin' about Ray tellin' me he had two hundred in his case, and ever since I been wonderin' if he planted the dough some place, or if it was stolen by someone who dun him in for it.'

14

A Business Proposition

'TWO HUNDRED QUID makes a tidy packet,' Lester said, sniffling. 'I thought about who might have took it, and if no one did, then where would Ray plant it? He had time to plant it, see! I got to workin' it out. It couldn't have been Mac, 'cos he'd have rushed off to the nearest pub. Harry, yes. Carney is shrewd, and he don't drink. Then there's George Barby. George is always careful of his money. He likes a drop, but not enough to blow two hundred on a bender.

'Then something happened what hit me to leg. It was about three weeks after Ray went off. I was repairing the fences round the horse paddock when a wire snapped back and gashed me arm. It bled a lot, and I came home for something to stop it. All hands were away, so I went over to the kitchen to get Ma Fowler to fix me arm properly. And when I walked into the annexe, them women was arguing in the kitchen, spittin' at each other like a coupla cats.

'Joan was saying that she didn't have any of the money, and that if Carney had found it he was keepin' it to himself. She goes on to say that it's more'n likely Mac dug it up somewhere, else where did he get the money to buy Ma that emerald ring. Ma threatened to smash Joan's face in if she bilked her for her share, and Joan laughs and says: if ever she did lay her hands on that twelve thousand five hundred quid her Ma would never know.

'They goes at it, and I'm quiet and listening in the annexe, and after a bit Joan says something about Ray's gold locket. Ma tells her to forget about the locket, saying it'll be many a year before anyone finds Ray Gillen. Joan says it'll be about a year before the Lake dries out, and first on the body gets the locket, and whoever gets the locket gets that twelve thousand five hundred of the best.

'With that Joan goes out of the kitchen and I cleared back to the pepper trees and went in again as though for the first time, and Ma Fowler doctored me arm. And sweet as sugar, she was.'

Lester's watery eyes encountered Bony's steady regard, and Bony nodded.

'It sorta come plain to me why them women and Carney and Mac always seem to be watching each other,' Lester said. 'I knew them four was up to something, and when I heard the women quarrelling I knew what about. I could never make out how the locket came into it, unless it was a sort of clue telling where Ray had planted his money.

'But the thing that stuck in me mind was the amount of

dough the women mentioned. I wrote it in words on a bit of paper. Then I wrote it in figures with the pound sign in front, and I knew I had seen them figures in a paper some time. I got a good memory for horses and performances and sporting dates, and I stewed over them figures for weeks before they hit me between the eyes.

'I could tell you where I seen them figures and when I seen 'em. I couldn't contact any names by them figures, but I remember suddenly the yarn told about 'em. There was two blokes up in Queensland what won £25,000 in a lottery, and they divi'd the cash between 'em in a pub bedroom. I musta read about it in a sportin' paper, 'cos I don't read no other kind except the sport pages.' Lester closed his eyes. 'I can see them figures now, Bony. £25,000 and some words I can't remember, and then £12,500, as plain as I can see you.'

'Are you telling me, Bob, that you believe Gillen had £12,500 in his case?' Bony prompted.

'I am, Bony. I am tellin' you just that. Look! Ray comes here from nowhere. Has a suitcase what he always keeps locked and the key around his neck. He gets worried when someone has a go at his case. He tells me he's got two hundred in it. Two hundred quid is a nice wad, but not so big that anyone here would of done him in for it. Even take it out of his case. But £12,500 is something, Bony.'

'I agree, but . . .'

'What?'

'A man would be a fool to get around with all that money in a suitcase.'

'Ray Gillen was a fool,' countered Lester.

'All right, then. But would he take a job here when he had all that money?'

'Yair. And I know why. He told me. His bike had broke down beyond Johnson's, and he walked here the next morning to get repairs. We was all out except the women. He was asked in for morning smoko. He seen Joan. So he asked Martyr for a job. He said so.'

'But £12,500!' Bony persisted, and Lester sniffled.

'Caw! Be your age. I carried a swag once with over four hundred quid and cheques for another two hundred in me hip pocket. Stormy Sam had a cigar-box in his swag when they come on his body up near Wilcannia. Full of opals and gold sovereigns and English bank-notes. And Sam died just naturally. I reckon Ray Gillen got suspicious and planted his money until he was fed up with Joan and ready to clear out.'

'What about the locket? How does that enter the picture?'

'I don't get the locket, Bony, and that's dinkum. But that locket is important to the women. They think it will lead 'em to the dough, which is why they're so interested in the Lake dryin' out, which is why Mac and Carney is so interested in the Lake, too. I reckon he planted his money and put 'em off somehow with a yarn about the locket. But they didn't get the money 'cos they're all still here ... waitin' for Lake Otway to die to find Ray's body. You help me find that money, and we go fifty-fifty.'

'You thought Gillen might have buried his money among the dead birds in the tank?'

'Yair,' replied Lester. 'Good place, too.'

'And you haven't an idea who waited for you to get out of that tank?'

'Too dark to see. Can't understand why he waited for me. I never seen him till after he punched me on the jaw. He picked me up like I was a bag and caught me on the side of me neck. He musta been there when I was forking out them birds, and he musta known I didn't chuck anything out before I got out meself. Pity the bloody fork didn't drop on him.'

'Perhaps he thought you had found the money and had it inside your shirt.'

'Could have.'

'Did he look when he had you down?'

'Don't know. I passed out. Musta been lyin' there a coupla hours before I come to. It was just breakin' day when I got back here and nutted out how I could explain me condition. I'd like to know which of 'em bashed me. I'd get him if I waited ten years.'

'Concentrate on the money,' urged Bony.

'Ain't I concentratin' on it?'

'How often did Gillen go riding on his bike?'

'How. ... Oh, pretty often of an evening. Usta take one or other of the women on the back.'

'Which direction, which track did he take?'

'Mostly to Johnson's Well.'

'What other track?'

'Don't recall he ever went another way. Sometimes he'd ride right round the Lake, keeping on the edge of the flats.' Lester sniffled, and Bony wished he wouldn't. 'I reckon I know what you're headed for, Bony. I thought he might have planted his dough at Johnson's Well 'cos he came here from Ivanhoe and he would prob'bly go back that way, pick up his money when passing the Well. There ain't a holler log, or a holler tree, I haven't delved into. I been down the Well, thinking he might have dropped a tin with the money in it and a wire hitched to the tin, or he might have planted it behind a board holding the shaft. I been up every tree round the Lake looking for a likely hole.'

'Then what about the Lake? The deepest part is at the Channel, isn't it?'

'Yes, but ...'

'If I wanted to plant money ... notes ... I'd stuff them into treacle tins which have press-on lids,' Bony said. 'The treacle tins I'd put into a twelve-pound cyanide tin which also has a press-on lid. The notes would be safe enough under water for twelve months.'

'Cripes, Bony, you got a head on you. Gillen knew about the Channel, of course. Diving for the tin of dough wouldn't stonker him. Funny if after he got drowned he was sorta steered about the Lake to drop into the Channel and be lying on top of his dough, guardin' it sort of.'

'Think it likely?'

'Could be. When Gillen was drowned, there was more'n twelve feet of water. Like a sea it was when the wind blew hard. You could hear the surf a mile away. The tide would go out along that side off where the wind blew and rise high on the opposite side. That set up currents. You could see the birds ridin' 'em. And Gillen never come ashore.'

'What d'you think prevented the body coming ashore?'

'Well, if he drowned, and he needn't, Ray was probably well out near the middle. But where he went down don't really matter, as I'll prove. Anyhow, he drowns in twelve feet of water. After three days up he comes. We're all waitin' for him to come ashore. He's like a small raft ... the middle of him 'cos his legs and his head is just under. If he was murdered and his body heaved into the Lake, it would float back upward: if he drowned, then he would float stummick up. His stummick would be the raft, get me?'

'Yes,' replied Bony.

'Then what happens? I'll tell you. The raft gives landing ground to the crows, and the crows goes for the belly. They always go for the belly of anything dead. The crows tear at the belly and lets out all the gas what made the body rise. With the gas out, the body sinks again.

'The body don't rest hard on the bottom, Bony. In the water he ain't got much weight, if any, so it just touches the mud. Then the currents moves it slowly round and about until it tangles with the old fence crossing the Lake or among the branches of one of the two red gums what fell long before the flood. Or it could have moved all over the place till it fell over the edge and down to the bottom of the Channel. You any good at swimming?'

'Not good enough to dive among a dead man's bones,' answered Bony with conviction.

'Me, neether,' Lester said. 'Still, twelve thousand of the best is worth a bit of horrer.'

'The water has receded from the two ancient trees,' Bony said.

'Yair, I know. The tops of the posts of the old fence showed up more'n a month ago. With me feet I prodded that fence from shore to shore feeling for Ray. He ain't tangled with the fence. Nor the trees. So he's in the Channel. Even if he wasn't drowned but bumped off and thrown in dead, he'd be in the Channel . . . ten or eleven feet down.'

Bony stood, saying:

'I'd better get back to my horses and turn them out. Too hot for work. I haven't been round the Lake for a week. When did you circle it last time?'

'More'n a week ago.'

'And the others? D'you know?'

'They give up going round her when the water went down and left the trees high and dry. I beat Carney to the fence-proddin' by a coupla nights.' Lester sniffled. 'I been watchin' all of 'em. They ain't missed much, especially Joan. Do we go fifty-fifty?'

Bony half sat on the veranda rail and rolled another cigarette. His back was towards the house, and he 'felt' green eyes and dark eyes boring into him. His answer to Lester's question was given with a nod.

'Good on you,' approved Lester. 'We work together. You get around the Lake as much as you can on your youngsters, just to make sure Ray ain't lying out in the sun. I'll keep my eyes on the others. They're thinkin' of the locket, and how they expect that to lead 'em to the dough beats me. Still, we got to keep ahead of 'em even with the locket. Then one night when the water's gone from both sides of the Channel, we'll do a bit of draggin'.'

Again Bony nodded.

'Then when we find the money we divi up, and I'm telling you we got to go careful when we do. No lashin' it out in the pubs. No buying flash cars and clothes or women. We spends it quiet like, slow, and steady, so nobody will wonder where we got a hell of a lot of cash and ask questions. Some I know would write to the income-tax bastards, and they would ask why, see?'

'Yes, I see,' admitted Bony. He moved from the rail and took a few steps from Lester. Then he turned about and asked:

'Where did you learn about bodies in water, and how they come up and what happens to them, Bob?'

Once again the sniffle mixed up with the chuckle.

'Sort of come to me through the family,' replied Lester. 'Me grandfather got the licence of a shanty on the river up near Bourke. Long time back, 'fore I was born. Then me old man took over the pub when the grandfather fell into the river one night and got drowned. Times were wild. Lots of cheque-men sort of fell into the river and was drowned. Me grandfather, an' me old man, often come on a dead body. Quite a cemetery growed around the pub, and they could tell what bodies was drowned and what wasn't.'

'Did you inherit the pub?' smilingly asked Bony.

'Not a chance. The old man drank hisself outer the pub in less'n eight years and went bullock-drivin'. Had a fight one day with another bullocky. With their whips, old style. The other bloke accidentally got his whip round the old man's throat and before he could get it clear the old man was a body, too. Terrible hard doer, the old man.'

That was the only occasion when Bony forgave Lester his sniffle.

15

Passing of Lake Otway

WHEN THE GROUND at foot was still hotter than the rays of the setting sun, they went down to the Lake . . . everyone, including the women. When the overseer and the two women had emerged from the house, the men had automatically joined them, as though magnetized by inevitability. No one spoke as they crossed the iron-hard flats to the softer marge which had been covered with water only that morning.

The pale-yellow solidified light that had been Lake Otway this last day of its existence was now a tarnished wafer of old gold, heavy, metallic, flat. Far outward from the 'shore' blemishes constantly appeared, dabs of darker-brown which moved to draw silver lines quickly erased. The divers couldn't dive any more, and they sat upon the metallic wafer like little china ducks, and here and there in grand but terrible isolation the ibis and the heron and the crane stood motionless as though dead.

Far out beyond them the ducks were congregated as the pelicans had gathered, and they waited for the leaders to take off along the sky-ways to far-away waters. Two cormorants perched atop the marker post, their wings drooping to dry as though in mockery of the Lake. The only note of joy in life was struck by the gulls who rode upon the golden wafer, high and clean and beautiful.

Bodies rested on the marge, bodies rested along the edge of the water, the countless bodies of fish. Beyond the dead fish the doomed sought frantically to evade the inevitable. Their broad backs were the dark dabs on the wafer of gold, their bodies drawing the silver lines upon it. The marker post no longer registered.

After the sun had gone the colour of Lake Otway swiftly changed, taking from the western sky its coating of crimson, and Mrs Fowler cried:

'Isn't it awful? It's like a plate of tomato soup.'

And MacLennon said:

'By this time tomorrow we'll be able to walk across without getting our boots muddy.'

Yet again the night came upwards from the ground. It turned the water to molten lead. It crept like a mist over the flats, about the feet of the watchers, dimming the greyish legs of the cranes. It drew everything down and down as though Earth and everything upon it was a hell being banished from the glory of the sky.

The sky was salmon-pink to the west, merging with emerald-green, passing to the blue of Bony's eyes down by the eastern horizon. They could not see the beginning of the bird migration, but through the rising night there came to the watchers the whirring of wings, faint and yet momentous. Then beneath the celestial canopy appeared the ducks in formations, moving fast and sure. The wading birds flap-flapped their way upwards, and the cormorants weaved about them. Presently only the gulls remained. The gulls hovered about the watchers like the ghosts of the departed.

'I'm going to the house,' Mrs Fowler decided, hysteria in her voice. 'I've had enough.'

She moved away through the rising night towards the bluff. The face of the bluff and the walls of the buildings were dove-grey, but the windows were oblongs of blood. Lester spoke, and the woman spun about as though struck.

'Tomorrer we'll be able to look around for Ray Gillen.'

'Why bring that up?' drawled Carney.

'Why not? We all been waitin' to find him, ain't we? Ray's somewhere about . . . what's left of him.'

'Don't count me in,' flashed Carney. 'I'm not interested in finding Ray Gillen. Never was. I had nothing to do with him . . . not like some people.'

'Well, you can all ride out tomorrow,' Martyr said, quietly. 'Gillen ought to be found and be decently buried. And then we ought to suffer less from bickering.'

Mrs Fowler hurried away, and the gulls fluttered after her, flew on beyond her and vanished against the dark face of the bluff. Bony felt a hand rest lightly on his forearm, and brought his gaze down to Joan's face.

'I didn't think the Lake would die like that,' she said, slowly 'It's left it all naked and stiff like a . . . like a real body.'

'You have seen a real body?'

'I read books, stupid.'

They proceeded to the bluff steps. He asked:

'What did Lester mean when he said everyone has been waiting for the Lake to dry out in order to find Gillen's body?'

'It's been in our minds for a long time,' replied the girl. 'You see, Ray Gillen was a ... he was hard to forget. If Lester or Mac had been drowned, we'd have forgotten all about them by now. Did you hear what Carney said?'

'That he isn't interested in finding Gillen's body, yes.'

'When he goes riding tomorrow you keep close by. He's interested all right. Ray used to wear a gold locket round his neck. Probably still there. Ray promised me that locket, and if Carney gets it he won't give it up. You get it and give it to me. Will you?'

'If he promised it to you,' Bony said, with assumed doubt.

'He did, I tell you. Now no more. But remember, that locket belongs to me.'

Having arrived at the steps hewn into the bluff face, she ran up them and was nowhere in view when Bony reached the top. Lights sprang up in the house and someone switched on the light in the men's quarters.

Bony found Carney already in the sitting-room settling down to read a magazine. Lester slumped into the arm-chair on the veranda, and Bony joined him to sit on the boards and roll a cigarette.

'Stinker of a night, ain't it?' Lester complained, and Bony agreed. 'Sort of night that dynamo engine gets on me nerves. Bang, bang, bang, right into me head.'

'I think I'll carry my bunk outside for the night,' Bony decided. 'Too hot in the room.'

'Good idea. You might give me a hand with mine. Set 'em up back of the building where they'll be in the shade first thing in the morning. Blasted heat-waves. Can't stand 'em like I usta. Hear how Carney bit just now when I said about huntin' for Gillen?'

'Methinks he doth protest too much.'

'Caw! You musta got that off Martyr. He knows a lot of them sayings. Puts 'em into his poetry, too.'

'He writes poetry?'

'Pretty good at it. You understand it?'

'Genuine poetry, yes.'

'Can't stand a bar of it.'

MacLennon appeared from the darkness.

'Took a screw at the thermometer,' he said. 'A hundred and three. In the shade! In the night! A hundred and three! Be a bitch of a day tomorrow.'

'We're sleeping outside,' Bony told him. 'Give me a hand with the beds?'

At break of day the flies woke every man, and Carney said he had had the bush and would quit.

'Better not,' advised MacLennon. 'Mightn't be safe.'

They glared at each other, and Carney, becoming angry, drawled:

'If I want to quit, I quit, Mac. What you might be thinking don't trouble me.'

'No? Well, go ahead and see what happens. No one quits on his own.'

'Yair, that's right,' interposed Lester. 'No one quits till we agrees on the divi.' The interjection appeared to calm the others. They both stared at Lester, and Carney said:

'It's up to you, Bob. Spill it.'

'Oh, no, it isn't. It's up to you or Mac.'

'Aw, what's the use,' snarled MacLennon. 'Shut up talkin' like kids. You goin' to work the horses in this heat, Bony?'

'This morning, anyway,' replied Bony. 'Mustn't let up on two I'm taking through the hoops. I'll put in a couple of hours before breakfast.'

They lapsed into sullen silence. Bony dressed and walked to the stables for the fed horse, and knew they watched him. The risen sun already burned his flesh when he rode out for the youngsters, and when the breakfast gong was struck no living thing voluntarily ventured from the shade.

'If only the wind would rise,' Carney said as, with Bony, he paused to look out over the Lake as they crossed to the annexe.

'If only to shoo the flies from pestering our eyes.' Bony heartily agreed. 'As you did this morning, I feel like quitting. Too hot to work. Might put in a week with George and the rabbits. That's not water down there. The water has vanished.'

'Yes. Bloody shame.'

The gleaming shield still covered Lake Otway, but now areas of mottled grey dulled the shield, and Bony fancied that, even as he watched, these areas were expanding. Following breakfast, he looked again at the Lake. Those grey areas were spreading fast as the last of the surface moisture was sucked up by the murderous sun.

At morning smoko, the temperature in the pepper tree shade was 117 degrees, and on Lake Otway there wasn't sufficient moisture to service a postage stamp.

Nevertheless, the depression wasn't yet hard enough to bear a horse, and Martyr had sent MacLennon out on a job, and he himself had taken Carney on the utility to work some miles away. Lester, who had been told to take life easy, was hugging the shade of the quarters veranda and reading a sporting paper when Bony rode off to visit George Barby.

He found the trapper had shifted camp to Johnson's Well, and that he had begun the erection of his fence around the Channel. Barby was cooking at a fire outside the hut when Bony arrived and neck-roped his horse to a shady tree.

'How's things?' shouted Barby. 'Come in out of the sun and have a cuppa tea.'

The dogs barked with no enthusiasm. The galah, perched on a biscuit tin, kept its beak wide open and panted, its wings drooping and reminding Bony of the cormorants. The cats watched Bony, their mouths wide and pink, and their flanks working like bellows. And Barby, lean and tough, was naked save for the towel tethered about his middle with string.

'Pretty flamin' hot, ain't it?' he said, pouring the 'cuppa' into a tin pannikin for his guest. 'Sugar on the truck. Bit of brownie in the box.'

'A hundred and seventeen when I left,' Bony told him.

'Don't talk about it. I give up labour. Even the blasted cats can't take it. Look at 'em. Got to nurse 'em. Watch!'

Taking the canvas water-bag from the hook suspended from the hut veranda, he stroked one of the cats and without difficulty persuaded it to lie flat on its back. Slowly he tipped the bag and poured the comparatively cool water on the animal's tummy, and the cat squirmed with pleasure and began to purr. In like fashion, he treated the other cat and, to Bony's amusement, the galah flopped off the biscuit tin and came staggering to them, wings trailing, beak wide with distress.

'If you think I'm goin' to keep on doing this all day, you're mistaken,' Barby protested.

The galah tumbled over its head to lie on its back like the cats. Barby scooped a rough hole in the sand and poured water into it. He held a finger low and the bird clasped it and suffered itself to be lifted and lowered into the hole, back downward. Then Barby sloshed water over it, and the bird sat up like an angry old man and swore. Then it lay down again and would have purred if able.

'Ruddy characters,' Barby claimed. 'Poor bastards, they can't stand this heat.' Genuine pity stirred his voice, and he tried to hide it by saying: 'There's seven or eight crows in that tree where you tied your horse. If it gets much hotter they're goin' to perform. You know who chucked all them birds out of that tank?'

'Should I?' countered Bony. 'When was it done?'

'Night before last. Anyone missing from the quarters night before last?'

'MacLennon, Lester, Carney.'

'What about Martyr?'

'I don't know about him,' Bony smiled. 'I mentioned to the men that the birds in the tank were to within a few inches of the top. It puzzled them, and Lester said they were not that high when he looked in some time ago.'

'Wonder what they expected to find,' chortled Barby. 'Money? Hell! Gillen? Perhaps. You got no idea who it was?'

'Lester. He was bashed on leaving the tank.'

Bony told of Lester's ruse to allay suspicion by saying he had been tossed, and Barby grinned.

'I knew it was Lester,' he said, triumphantly. 'I was over here at sun-up yesterday morning, getting drinkin' water, and right against the tank I found his old beret. He never went anywhere after dark without it. So Bob Lester can't know where Ray Gillen's money is planted. Wonder why they bashed him.'

'You don't know who bashed him?'

Barby's dark eyes were abruptly hard.

'No. Think I should?'

'As I see it, George, Carney and Mac followed Lester. They waited for him to empty the tank. When he jumped out, one of them bashed him ... hard enough to knock him out for several hours. Doesn't it appear to you that Carney and

MacLennon both were after the money and thought it possible that Lester found it among the dead birds?'

'Looks like it, don't it?'

'Therefore, Carney and MacLennon also cannot know where Gillen's money is.'

'H'm!' grunted the trapper. 'Bit of a mix-up, eh?'

16

Smoke on the Bluff

'ANYTHING MORE BEEN said about the gun going off?' Barby asked, when they were eating lunch.

'Not a word,' Bony replied. 'You make a good curry, George.'

A bag nailed to the window-frame of the hut would have darkened its interior against the flies, but the heat within was unbearable. They defeated the flies by making a smoke fire in the shade cast by the hut and squatting on their heels either side this small fire to envelop their heads and the meal within smoke.

'Only tucker worth eating this weather,' Barby said. 'I been thinking about that gun, and where it went off, and what was workin' up. Something or other will bust before long. You got any idea where that money could of been hid?'

'Afraid not. It wasn't buried among those dead shags.'

Had Bony been able to forget he was a horse-breaker, Barby quite unconsciously would have repeatedly reminded him, for deep inside the English Barby was ever the superiority towards the 'native'. It was Barby's opinion that his own intelligence and powers of reasoning were far higher than that of the heathen, and this attitude amused and gratified Bony because it cloaked his work as a criminal investigator.

'I see you are going to trap the Channel,' he said, casually.

'Yair. I done a bit to the fence along one side and the trap, and I'll finish this evening and start. What about coming in with me?'

'I'd like to. Seems to me you could do with twenty assistants.'

'I could do with fifty.' Barby tossed his tin plate to the ground and groped for the pannikin of tea. 'You and me together can't deal with the mob of rabbits round here. We couldn't trap 'em and skin 'em fast enough to beat the sun. Then there's millions right round the Lake what'll be headed this way tonight for water. All we can do is skin what we can.'

'The 'roos are going to be a nuisance to your fence,' Bony reminded him. 'Any guns with your gear?'

'Couple of Winchesters and a twelve-bore shot-gun. We'll have to sit up most of the night to keep 'em off the fence. Got plenty of ammo, fortunately. Blast! It's hot, ain't it. Don't remember being so hot for years.'

Bony washed the utensils and Barby crossed to the trough and let water gush into it from the reservoir tank. The dogs loped over to him and plunged into the trough. He brought a bucket of water back to the hut shade, scooped a hole, splashed water into it, and the two cats lay in the water and rolled in the wet sand after the water had soaked away. The galah demanded attention and was given a wet hole all to itself.

Bony sat with Barby, their backs to the hut wall and with gum-tips whisked the flies from the their faces. Barby explored the possibilities of generating power from the sun's heat, and climaxed the subject by asserting that the capitalists would never allow it.

'D'you think the scientists will ever make rain when they want to?' he asked.

'Quite likely,' replied Bony.

'If they do, they'll ruin Australia,' predicted the trapper. 'What keeps the rabbits down, and the foxes, and the blowflies, and the kangas? What d'you reckon?'

'The droughts.'

'Course. If it wasn't for the ruddy droughts no white man could live in the country, and the remainin' blacks would migrate to Blighty. Myxotitis! Rot! Just as well spray the rabbits with hair oil.'

'It seems you wouldn't like the rabbits to be wiped out,' dryly observed Bony.

'Because why? There's hundreds of blokes making a good

living outa rabbits and the fur, and while rabbits run there's no excuse for any man to be out of work in Australia. I know trappers what take live rabbits into country where there ain't any, just to let 'em breed up. Why not? Done it meself, but don't you ever tell the Boss.'

Bony laughed.

'The Boss would be annoyed?'

'He'd drop dead,' Barby agreed and chuckled. The mood passed, and the note of indignation crept back into his voice.

'Fancy wiping out all the rabbits what give rich women albino fox furs and coats, and Kohinoor mink and Alaskan capes and things. Fancy killing all the rabbits what could give cheap meat to the working people who got to pay four bob for a pound of measly mutton chops. And just to let farmers buy more cars and crash-bang boxes for the kids. And dirty politicians putting more and more racket money down south in wads we couldn't lift off the ground.'

Bony thought it was hot enough without becoming worked up over a mixture of economics and politics, but the wads neither Barby nor he could lift off the ground spurred imagination, and imagination did help to make the heat bearable. Lucky politicians.

'Yair,' continued Barby. 'Something wrong somewhere. Old age pensioners freezing all winter in their one rooms down in the stinkin' cities, and the politicians rushing round the world on holiday trips we pay for. They calls it the March of Science. What's science done for us, anyhow? Me and you's still stuck here in this flaming joint, and millions of workers still got to toil day and night for a crust. Australia! Look, Australia would be the finest country in the world if it wasn't for the morons running it.'

'Agreed, George, agreed,' murmured Bony. 'Do you happen to see what I see?'

Bony pointed to the low dune barring the Lake from the creek. Beyond the dune a stark pillar of smoke appeared like a fire-blackened tree supporting a snow-white cloud. Together they stood, and without speaking walked to the dune, oblivious of the sun on exposed arms and the heat striking up from the ground through their boots.

The base of the smoke column was shot with crimson.

'Don't remember seeing any fire alarm, I suppose?' queried

Barby, his voice thin. 'Better hop into the ute and light our fags at the last ember.'

They shifted unnecessary dunnage from the utility. The dogs were chained. The galah was thrust into its cage. The horse was left in the shadow of the cabbage tree. Without undue speed, Barby drove the oven-hot vehicle over the sandy track to the homestead.

'Who was there when you left?' he asked.

'Lester and the two women.'

'Would've made no difference if there'd been a hundred men about the place,' Barby said. 'All pretty old buildings. Bit of a spark . . . pouf . . . few ashes . . . all in two minutes . . . day like this.'

They passed through low scrub and over ragged ridges and the world was utterly still and strangely stereoscopic, the only movement being the twisting column ahead. They saw that the quarters were safe, and the tops of the pepper trees were thrashing in the updraught created by the red remains of the large house. The machinery shed and the store and other buildings were warped but not ignited.

Lester they found bending over someone sitting in the armchair on the veranda of the quarters. He didn't notice the arrival of the utility, or of the travellers until they stepped up to the veranda and Barby said:

'You been tryin' to singe the flies, Bob?'

Lester straightened, and they saw the occupant of the chair was Joan. Lester's face was drawn by obvious shock, and he forgot to sniffle.

'Yair,' he said. 'Ma got caught.'

The girl stared at the smouldering ruin, her hands pressed between her knees. As though whimpering she said:

'I couldn't get her out. I tried . . . I couldn't.'

'I was sitting here having a cat-nap,' Lester put in. 'I hear a roar and I thinks it's a willi passing by, till Joan run over and woke me up. Then the ruddy house was going up swoosh, and there wasn't a chance to get near it. Burned faster than dead buckbush in hell.'

'It would in a shade temperature of 117 degrees,' agreed Bony, and Lester snorted without sniffling.

'Hundred and seventeen!' he echoed. 'A hundred and twenty-one when I came back from lunch.'

'No one else home?' asked Bony, who had unconsciously taken command of the situation.

Lester shook his head. Joan repeated her whispered statement, then she sat upright and looked dazedly at Bony.

'I was reading in my room, and Mum was lying down in her room. All of a sudden I was surrounded by smoke and flames. I ran to Mum's room, but she had fainted or something, and I dragged her off the bed, but I had to leave her. The house was crashing . . . I couldn't stop with her.'

Smoke stains and ash streaked her face and arms. As she continued to stare at the ruins, Bony turned her chair from the picture of desolation. Her hands remained clasped between her knees as though to control their trembling, and he left her to procure aspirin and water.

'Take these,' he said, his voice hard in an effort to defeat possible hysteria. 'Bob, boil a billy and brew some tea. Make it strong.' The girl swallowed the tablets obediently. Gently Bony patted her shoulder. 'Cry if you can, Joan. It'll help.'

He left Barby with her. Lester was making a fire behind the building. He crossed to the machinery shed, noted how close it and the store had come to destruction. The smoke column was now a thin spiral, and high in the sky the smoke had solidified to a huge white cloud. Wherever the overseer was, he must see that cloud.

Of the house nothing remained bar the roof iron now lying upon the grey ash. Even the three chimneys had collapsed. He was able to draw close enough to see the remains of the iron bedsteads and their wire mattresses, the cooking range and several iron pots and boilers, the piping carrying the power lines, the steel safe where the office had been.

Joan Fowler was fortunate to have escaped, for certainly she would have been given no more than a few seconds to get out of the inferno.

It occurred to him that the heat of the ruin was barely higher than the heat of the sun. There was no doubt concerning the abnormal heat of the early afternoon, and he could imagine the temperature within the house before the fire started. Even the bedrooms would be like fired ovens, and to lie on a bed, fully dressed, would be an ordeal. Joan had said she was reading in her room when smoke and flame surrounded her, and that her mother was lying in her bedroom.

That worried him as he sauntered about the huge oblong of grey ruin which had been a house.

On the far side of the site the few citrus trees were beyond salvation, and the garden was destroyed. At the bottom of the garden stood the fowl-house, intact, and within the netted yard were the bodies of several hens. Their white shapes drew Bony. He wondered if they had been killed by the heat of the sun or the heat of the fire. His own throat was already stiff with thirst.

Farther on beyond the garden fence grew an ancient red gum. It stood on the slope of the bluff and when Bony went on to the fence he was out of sight of those on the veranda of the men's quarters. There was a gate in the fence, and he wasn't mistaken by that which had drawn him to it. On the red ground was a gold ring set with sapphires. It lay in the half-moon depression made by the heel of a woman's shoe, and because, as always, he had noted and memorized the tracks of everyone living here, he knew that the impression had been made by Joan when returning through the garden to the house, from one of the two house lavatories.

These structures were farther down the slope and fifty yards apart. The imprints on the path leading to each revealed which of these was used solely by the women.

He retrieved the sapphire ring, and remembered having seen this ring worn by Mrs Fowler. He recalled that Joan was now wearing her lounge clothes, a jewelled bow in her hair. Also that she was wearing the wristlet watch given her by Lester, and an opal bracelet thought by Witlow to have been subscribed by Martyr.

He followed the path to the lavatory visited by the women. Behind the door, suspended from a hook, was an old and shabby handbag, and as he examined the contents his eyes were hard and his mouth grim. There was a lipstick in a studded holder; a gold-etched compact and cigarette-case; a few bobby pins; a bank-book in Joan Fowler's name showing a credit of £426 6s.; and a roll of treasury notes bound with darning wool. And a gold brooch set with opals, an emerald ring, and a wristlet watch.

The jewellery belonged to the late Mrs Fowler.

17

After the Fire

BONY RETURNED THE items to the handbag and the bag to its nail behind the door. He crossed to the other toilet, found nothing, and detoured to arrive at the pepper trees behind the outbuildings. The dogs welcomed him, unconscious of their good fortune, unaware of the effect of the fire upon the upper portion of the trees. He spoke to them, patted several, and passed round to the front to regard with studied interest the warped walls and doors of the machinery shed and other buildings. Like a man shocked by the catastrophe, he wandered to the edge of the hot ruin, remained for a while, and finally joined Lester and Barby, with Joan Fowler, on the quarters veranda.

They barely noticed him, each seemingly engrossed by a private problem. Lester had brewed tea, and Bony helped himself and squatted on his heels to roll and smoke a cigarette. Presently Barby said:

'No hope of phoning to the homestead, I suppose?'

'Don't think,' replied Lester. 'There was a coupla spare instruments, but they were inside the office when I last seen 'em.'

'Where did Martyr go?'

'Went out to Winter's Mill with Carney. Took the ute.'

'Take 'em an hour and a half to get home . . . after they seen the smoke,' Barby estimated. 'Just as well make ourselves comfortable.'

'Can't we get Mum out of that?' complained Joan, and wasn't answered till she repeated her remark.

'She ain't feelin' nothing,' Lester pointed out. 'Hell, it's hot, all right. Couldn't be worse droving a mob of rams on the plains. What d'you reckon, George? Reckon Martyr'll take the lot of us to the River homestead?'

'Don't think. Take Joan in, of course.'

'Go to the River!' the girl exclaimed. 'I'm not leaving here.'

The suggestion banished the lethargy of shock, and her

eyes blazed at Barby as though he dictated her future. He stroked his moustache with the mouth of his pipe and regarded her, calmly frigid.

'There's no argument. I'm not the Boss.'

'But why should I leave here?' persisted the girl. 'I'll be all right. I can cook here when you bring things from Sandy Well to cook with. Besides, I'm not leaving Mum . . . like that.'

Barby got up from the packing-case, and strolled into the sunlight and over to the smouldering ash. The girl watched him under partially lowered lids, her mouth twitching and her hands never still. Now and then the light was caught by the jewelled hair-clip and opal bracelet. Abruptly, she stood, and, as abruptly, Lester stood, too.

'Better not go over, Joan,' he advised. 'Better stay here. Nothink to see over there, anyhow. Ash'll cover up everything.'

'I . . .' Joan resumed her chair, and Bony knew she was as surprised as he was by the revelation of Lester's mental strength under crisis. Lester refilled the pannikins, and presently Barby came back. He nodded acceptance of the tea, stirred it with the splinter of wood serving as a spoon and sat upon his heels with the ease of the native-born. And the girl waited a long time before she burst out with:

'Well, did you see anything of Mum?'

'Pipe down, Joan,' snarled Barby. 'Nothing to see. Think about something pleasant, can't you?'

'No, I can't, and don't talk to me like that, George.'

'Got to, Joan, or you'll start a tantrum, and then I'll have to slap you out of it. It's too hot to argue.'

'Well, I'm not going to leave here, no matter what Martyr says.'

She looked at each of them as though hoping they would argue with her. Lester sniffled and snorted noisily. Barby seemed interested in the last spiral of smoke rising straight and slowly from the twisted iron sprawled upon the ground like the backs of sleeping beasts. Bony pretended to doze. It seemed hours before they heard the returning utility.

Martyr stopped his truck at the machinery shed, and he and Carney remained in it as they stared at the débris. Those on the veranda waited and watched, until the overseer and

Carney left the vehicle and walked to the edge of the ashes. They stayed there for several minutes before Martyr came to the quarters. His light-grey eyes were steel discs in his weathered face.

'How did it happen?' he asked.

'Don't know,' replied Lester. 'I was having a shuteye after lunch. I heard what I thought was a passing willi-willi, and took no notice until Joan shook me awake and I seen her going up . . . the house, I mean.'

'Mrs Fowler?'

'She got caught.'

The light-grey eyes turned to the girl, concentrated on her for a second, seemed to leap away from her to Barby, and returned to Joan. 'Tell me about it,' he said, and the girl faltered:

'I ran to her room. I tried to drag her out. She was in a faint or something, or unconscious from the smoke. I got her off her bed, but I couldn't get her out of her room. The place was full of flames all round. She was too heavy, and I couldn't breathe. I . . . We must get her out of that.'

Martyr sat on the case. Carney leaned against one of the veranda posts, his face blank but his brown eyes nervous. The girl lay back in the arm-chair, her eyes closed, restless fingers rotating the opal links of her bracelet. The men waited for the overseer, who apparently needed time to plan action. And Bony felt rather than witnessed growing elation in him.

'It's a rotten mess,' Martyr said in his terse manner. 'How much spare tucker have you, George?'

'Enough for a couple of days, but flour only for tomorrow,' replied Barby, anticipating the questioner's mind.

'Where are you camped?'

'Johnson's.'

'Take the men back with you. You fellows roll your swags and camp with George.' A faint smile flickered about Martyr's mouth. 'Give George a hand with the rabbits tonight . . . to earn your tucker. Harry, fill the ute tank and look to the oil. Joan, you'll come with me to Sandy Well, and then on to the River.'

'But why?' Joan sprang to her feet. 'I'm all right here. I can cook here instead of Mum.'

'What in? What clothes? What'll you cook?'

The girl's eyes grew big and almost baleful. There was nothing of resignation in her, or supplication. Carney stilled against his veranda post to watch her with admiration, her head flung back, breasts lifted high and her green eyes flashing. Bony thought of Boadicea.

'What in?' she shrilled. 'A pair of Mac's spare pants and one of your silk shirts.'

'My silk shirts are fired to ash.'

'Then Lester can lend me one. What's it matter? You bring back some cooking things from Sandy Well. And flour and rations. I'll manage to cook on the open hearth of the sitting-room. I'm not leaving, I tell you.'

'All right, Martyr said slowly and with emphasis. 'But you are not staying here. You can go with the fellows to Johnson's Well, and you can damn well do the cooking there. There's no window to the hut and the door won't shut, but no one will mind that. I'm sure. Come on, Harry. Help me fuel the ute and I'll get going to Sandy Well and the telephone. I'll leave you to see that Joan goes to Johnson's. And no fighting over her before I get back with the Boss and the police.'

Save for Carney, who crossed to the utility, they presented a tableau. The girl defiant, her mouth curved upwards; the overseer silently taunting her to stick to her guns; Lester and Barby waiting with cynical tensity for her final choice.

'That'll do me,' she said, and Martyr turned and walked after Carney.

Ten minutes, and the utility was served, and the overseer returned to the quarters, to address the men.

'No one is to interfere with the remains of the house, you understand. As soon as practicable. Sergeant Mansell will be out from Menindee, and he'll be in charge. That's the drill.'

'Righto, Mr Martyr,' Lester said and sniffled before adding: 'We'll get along.'

The overseer cogitated, regarding each of them in turn, coming in the end to Joan Fowler and staying with her a fraction longer than necessary.

'Wait for Mac, George, before you push off,' he said, and turned away.

He backed into the utility, slammed the door, started the

engine. They watched the dust rising behind the wheels as it sped up the long rise, and no one spoke till after the machine disappeared over the distant crest dancing in the heat. Carney sat on the veranda step and rolled a cigarette. Lester appeared to expect to see the utility reappear and come speeding down the rise. Bony drank more tea.

It was not a situation the girl could stand. She jumped to her feet, and Carney swung round to look at her.

'Well, if you all won't talk, I've something to do,' she said, almost shouting, and made to pass Carney.

'You heard what Martyr said,' Carney quietly reminded her. 'No interfering with the fire ashes.'

'Damn you, Harry! And the fire ashes, too. Let me pass. You can come with me if you like . . . right to the door.'

Carney was young enough to blush his embarrassment, but he managed a chuckle and airily replied that such a walk would be fine. The others watched them skirt the house site, to pass beyond the back of the bluff and towards the lower garden gate. When Carney's head only was in sight, he stopped and the girl went on. Lester sniggered, and Barby pointed out MacLennon, who was arriving at the yards.

MacLennon didn't dismount. He rode on to the quarters, astonishment depicted clearly on his unshaven, broad face.

'Someone play bonfires?' he asked.

'Yair,' replied Lester.

'Thought the wild blacks had attacked the joint,' MacLennon remarked, with ill-disguised casualness. Slipping off the sweat-drenched horse, he tethered the reins to the veranda rail, and almost fell upon the tea billy. 'What a bloody day! Anyone under the iron?'

'Ma Fowler.'

'You don't say, Bob! You shove her back in after the fireworks started?'

'S'far as I know, she never got out to be shoved back in,' Lester drawled. 'I was having a shut-eye when Joan woke me up with the news.'

'Where's she?'

'Over in the Little Bungalow. Harry took her halfway.' MacLennon put down the empty billy-can, wiped his mouth with a forearm, regarded Lester with sombre eyes, and Lester added hastily: 'Martyr said none of us was to go delving for Ma. Harry's seeing to it that Joan don't do no delving, see?'

'D'you think you're gonna stop me doing a bit of delving?' enquired MacLennon.

'Caw, blimey!' exploded Barby. 'Pipe down, you blokes. What's rasping you all the time? A woman gets burned up in a fire, and it's a police job. You got brains, I suppose. Martyr's gone for help, and tucker, and other things . . . including the Boss and the police. And you're all coming over to camp at my place.'

Bony slipped into his room, selected a few things and rolled his blankets into a swag. He dropped the swag outside the bedroom window, climbed after them, carried it to Barby's utility. He was 'meandering' about the machine shed when Carney and Joan returned to the quarters, and when the men were rolling swags for the move, he slipped away down the shoulder of the bluff and so to the 'Little Bungalow'.

The handbag behind the door was empty.

He emerged from behind the line of partially burned pepper trees when Lester and Carney brought their dunnage from the quarters to the utility and MacLennon was freeing his horse, and he was confident that none of them had been observing him.

Carney loosed the dogs, and they raced the horse to the trough. Bony was first aboard the truck, standing immediately behind its cabin on that side where Joan would enter. He was thus able to look down at her when she drew near and when she was about to step into the cabin. She was wearing a blouse of cream pleated silk, now soiled by smoke and ash. The plunging neckline, as he had anticipated, revealed a glimpse, nestling deep down, of the blue bank-book he had seen in the old handbag.

It was ten to five. The water-saturated dogs loped behind the vehicle which Barby drove unhurriedly. Nothing else stirred in all the land, the invisible host of rabbits crouching in shade and burrow, the invisible birds clinging to the shadows falling upon branches and even upon the ground. Nothing else moved but the eyes of watchful kangaroos, and the sky was void save for the watching, waiting eagles.

It was a relief to gain the comparative dimness of the trees about Johnson's Well, where they were welcomed by Barby's dogs and his now vociferous galah. Bony jumped to the ground immediately the truck stopped. With a flourish, he opened the door for Joan Fowler.

'Welcome to the bandits' lair, my lady!' he cried, and bowed.

Her clouded eyes widened, brightened. She smiled, wanly. As she stepped from the utility, he moved swiftly to offer a helping hand. The act was spoiled, for he tripped, lurched slightly, almost fell against her. Their hands missed contact, and his palm was pressed against her breast.

'Forgive my clumsiness,' he pleaded gravely. 'I hope I did not hurt you.'

The suspicion leaping in her eyes was beaten back. He was so confused, so contrite, so damn silly like all men. She smiled again, graciously.

He wondered if the jewellery he had felt inside her blouse had hurt her.

18

The Riddle of the Safe

THE TENSION CONTROLLING these men had broken during the short journey from the homestead, and for the first time they appeared to Bony as normal individuals. Lester sniffled and chortled and swore at the dogs, who were threatening Barby's dogs; MacLennon even laughed when Carney suggested bathing in the troughs, and George Barby waved to the hut and invited Joan Fowler to take possession.

Joan presented a character facet which might have astonished anyone other than these bushmen ... and they were gratified. She looked into the hut and walked round it. She studied the position of Barby's camp fire, and the contents of his tucker box she surveyed with marked contempt. She looked at the salt-encrusted meat-bag hanging from the branch of a nearby tree, and finally inspected the men, who had paused as though for orders.

'You think again if you're thinking all this is going to beat me,' she said. 'You thought I'd weaken when Martyr slung me into this. Thought you'd get rid of me, didn't you? What a hope! All you can offer me is a couple of clean blankets and a clean suit of pyjamas. And if you have a clean pair of trousers, Harry, I'll borrow them. A skirt and scanties won't do here.'

No one argued. Bony assisted Carney to carry the bedstead, brought from the quarters, to set up at the far side of the hut. Barby carried the mattress, and Carney supplied two blankets which happened to be comparatively new. Lester tore the dirty covering off a feather pillow and expertly covered it with one of Barby's snowy cooking aprons. They even placed a wool-pack on the ground beside the bed to serve as a mat. With unspoken mutual consent, they left it to Harry Carney to conduct the girl to 'her room'.

It was after five o'clock, and seemed to be even hotter than at noon. When removing the horse's neck-rope from the tree, Bony glanced upwards into its shadowy arches and saw the mynah birds and several crows, every beak wide agape, every wing drooping as though to permit a cooling draught of air to reach their breasts. He said nothing of his intention to ride the horse back to the homestead and release it in its own paddock.

It was too hot to ask the animal even to canter.

Human reactions to the destruction of the homestead he reviewed with calm detachment, and found himself now rather in the role of spectator than of director, for he had been content to watch human reactions and unfolding events and evade interference.

Excepting for that one incident of prodding the suspects by focusing interest in the tank filled with dead birds.

There could be no better example of stirring lethargic suspects than the destruction by fire of the homestead, for this event exerted strong influence on minds as well as the circumstances governing the lives of these people. And Bony experienced neither regret nor jealousy that he had not been the agent.

As the horse carried him at a fast walk, itself anxious for freedom and a drink, Bony surveyed the results of the fire upon all those vitally concerned. To begin with, the overseer.

Hitherto, Richard Martyr had appeared to be reticent, aloof, moody, given to introspection and far too much exercise of imagination. Then, being confronted by the ruin of the homestead, instead of dismay, even rage, because of carelessness, he had betrayed elation.

The effect of the fire hadn't been manifested in the others until they reached Johnson's Well, when they welcomed the change of living conditions. That was out of focus, because stockmen do not welcome a change from homestead food and homestead comfort to a rough camp where they would have to sleep on the ground and battle with the flies for stew on a tin plate, or kangaroo steak on a slab of baking-powder bread.

The reason for their satisfaction, Bony thought, was that they were still free to watch each other and hunt for the remains of Gillen.

The determination displayed by the girl not to leave these men was one of several interesting pointers in the progress of the human drama being played against the drama of the death of Lake Otway. Her possession now not only of her own bank-book and jewellery, but also of her mother's jewellery, proved that she had placed them in the old handbag behind the door of the toilet which no male would enter.

That collection had been made and secured before the house caught fire, and had been retrieved by Joan Fowler after the house had burned to the ground.

'You know, Starface,' he said to the horse, 'despite this devastating heat, I'm quite enjoying myself. A nice little cheque for training you and your friends added to my salary, plus the antics of half a dozen men under the influence of green eyes, plus the phenomenon of a dying lake to encourage my interest in natural history, combine to make me look upon criminal investigation as a lost cause.

'I ask myself, why wrestle with a problem which others will ultimately solve for me? All I need do to earn my salary is to wait upon events, because the Spirit of Drama impels the actors to play their cues. A comfortable attitude to duty, don't you think, Starface?'

They emerged from the dune scrub and took the last slope to the homestead bluff. The upper portion of the pepper trees marred the now familiar view, but only this scar was evident, for the fire ruin lay beyond the men's quarters. The windmill was still, had been for days. The unmistakable silence of the abandoned received Bony, and made the horse restive. It was at this moment that Bony saw the dust mist.

It lay like a brown fog atop the ridge where passed the track to Sandy Well and the River, and it had certainly been produced by the passing of a motor vehicle. Martyr's utility had raised dust at that place one hour earlier this afternoon, and the dust now hovering above the ridge could not possibly have lingered for so long a period.

Bony unsaddled and slipped the bridle, knowing the horse would find feed after drinking at the mill trough, and having stowed the gear in the harness room, he strode to the veranda of the quarters and there recalled the exact movements of Richard Martyr from the moment he arrived in the utility until he left in it for Sandy Well and the telephone . . . one hour earlier.

He then proceeded to check and prove that Martyr had returned to the homestead after everyone had departed in Barby's utility, and that he had left for the second time shortly following Bony's departure from Johnson's Well. Thus the reason for Martyr's return was quickly established.

The office safe had been moved, probably stood upright, and then replaced as formerly. It was situated four yards in from the edge of the bed of grey ash, and it was plain to Bony that the overseer had attempted to obliterate his tracks on the ash bed by blowing ash into them, using his broad-brimmed hat to create the draught.

Heat caused by the fire would now be negligible, but the safe was exposed to the sun and not to be handled with bare hands. Bony had to procure an empty sack to protect his hands and having memorized its position, he stood it up, when he found that the key was in the lock and, like the safe, bore plainly the effect of fire. Bony turned the key, and the door was easily swung open. The condition of the contents was a compliment to the safe maker. There was a stock book, a ledger, a time book, and taxation stamp sheets. In a small compartment were treasury notes, a little silver and taxation stamps. In the second compartment was the out-station work diary.

Bony relocked the safe, leaving the key in the lock. There

was no doubt that the key had been in the lock when the house burned, indicating that the safe hadn't contained anything of great value, and, therefore, what had brought Martyr back to open it and take pains to obliterate his tracks over the ash bed?

Having turned the safe to its original position, Bony scattered ash over its topmost side and, as Martyr had done, whisked ash over his tracks when retreating to the clear ground. The following ten minutes he spent studying the ruins and decided against delving among them. He did circle the ruins twice, hunting for traces having the slightest significance; finding none save those left by the overseer.

Martyr's examination of that safe nagged him, and he wished he knew if the overseer had returned to it to correct an omission of duty, such as to report the condition of the contents to his employer, or if he had purposely delayed the examination until all hands were cleared to Johnson's Well.

A cawing crow recalled the passing of time, the approach of evening. The sun was westering, and its decreasing heat was now permitting the birds to venture from the shadows to slake their day-long thirst. He must not remain here longer if he was to prevent suspicion, and while crossing to the quarters to obtain a packet of tobacco from his room his mind tore at the covering of this mystery.

What had brought Martyr back to his office safe? What had occurred to make the hands so cheerful, especially Lester? And why had Joan Fowler so strenuously rebelled against leaving Lake Otway, now dead? And why the defiant front following her arrival at Johnson's Well?

He sat on his stripped bed to open the packet of tobacco and roll a cigartete. He stood on the veranda smoking and hesitant to hurry back to Barby's camp. He gazed long at the rising land-swell and at its summit where he had seen the faint dust fog raised by the overseer's second departure. Nothing moved on that shadow-etched track.

Lester! Lester had been comforting the girl when Barby and himself had come. The girl had been sitting in the armchair, dabbing at her stained face.

That tableau could have been an act.

Lester! Bony entered Lester's room. He moved the mattress, finding between it and the wire under-mattress a ready-made suit layered between newspapers and kept there for pressing. Under the bed was a small tin trunk, its lock broken, its interior holding a jumble of old clothes, new town shoes, a horse bridle and books devoted to racing statistics. Also under the bed were old boots and, hard against the wall, a paper-wrapped parcel. He removed the string, opened one end and felt with sensitive fingers the notes compressed to wads.

The parcel was about the size of that made up for him by the bank manager at Brisbane. There was neither name nor mark on the outside of the wrapping paper. The wrapping might yield fingerprints. He put the parcel in a saddlebag on Gillen's motor-bike.

Passing down the bluff steps to gain the flats, he followed the old shore line, his mind tearing at several facets presented by these two developments . . . the fire and the fortune in notes under Lester's bed. First the fire. The fact that Joan Fowler had collected her own valuables, and also her mother's jewellery, and concealed them in a safe place to preserve them from destruction strongly indicated that she knew the homestead would be destroyed, and also that her mother would perish in the fire, or her mother's body would be consumed by the fire.

Following the fire, she had collected the valuables from the hiding place. That clearly indicated forethought, planning. Had Joan been in possession of the parcel of notes, would she not have hidden it in that safest of safe places . . . the women's toilet? Subsequently, however, she could not have thrust the parcel down inside her blouse, and it seemed feasible to assume that she had taken Lester in as an accomplice-in-part. She could have told Lester that she had escaped the fire with the parcel of money, not mentioning to Lester her mother's jewellery.

Secondly, Gillen's money. When in possession of twelve thousand pounds or more, would Joan Fowler have bothered about her mother's jewellery worth not more than two hundred pounds? Wearing her own jewellery after lunch, and when the fire began, she could explain, and be believed, by saying she had dressed for the afternoon, and had put on all her trinkets, really as something to distract her mind from the heat. Would she be silly enough, when possessed of twelve thousand pounds, to risk her mother's jewellery being associated with her escape from the burning house?

There was a fact not to be denied.

The parcel of notes under Lester's bed was free of the dust which lay upon the trunk and the other odds and ends, proving that the parcel had not been under the bed for more than a day or two at most.

Despite the annoying flies that seemed anxious to drown in his eyes and burrow into his ears, a slow smile stole over Bony's sharply-moulded features, and aloud he said:

'It seems, Detective-Inspector Bonaparte, that you will now have to work.'

19

The Channel Trap

BARBY ADOPTED THE plan of trapping rabbits at water holes and dams, and the construction of his fences and traps was much more intricate than the wide-wing fences he had built on the Lake flats.

The entire Channel was enclosed with wire netting and here and there the wire was brought to a point facing the water, an opening at the point being made to permit rabbits to squeeze through. Thirst-crazed rabbits thus able to reach the water and take their fill could not retreat by the way they had come, and when searching for the way of escape would find it in an outward-pointing V inside one of the two large netted yards.

Bony arrived in good time to contribute his labour ... physical ... to the work of building the Channel trap. The men worked with good will. What energized them? What drove them despite the heat? Barby's offer of a fair division of the 'catch' had its influence, but this was over-shadowed by the sporting instinct. Even Lester, with thousands of pounds under his bed, worked like a slave.

The job done, Barby went off to see how Joan was getting on with the cooking, saying he would bring her and

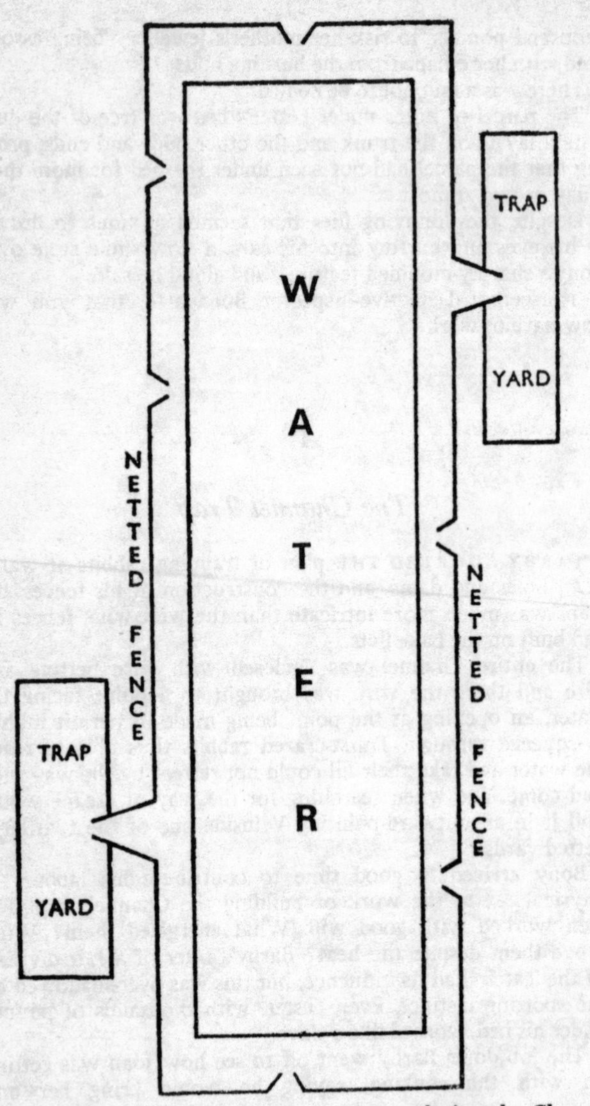

Plan of Barby's netted fence and traps enclosing the Channel

refreshments, 'to be in at the finish'. The others sat on the low mound spanning the mouth of the creek, and rolled smokes and tried to evade the glare of the sun striking at them across the great depression.

'I still reckon George oughta been satisfied to fence only one side of that water and have only the one trap,' MacLennon argued. 'If all the 'roos I've seen this last two weeks arrive here tonight, the ruddy fence will be flattened.'

'Have a try and keep 'em off,' Carney said in his easy manner. 'We've plenty of guns and ammo.'

'Yair,' agreed Lester. 'By midnight them traps should be two big blocks of fur.' He sniffled . . . as Bony knew he would. 'Give George a job skinning 'em. Last him a week at least. When we goin' to look for Ray Gillen?'

Easy attitudes visibly stiffened. Following a loaded silence, MacLennon asked:

'You in a hurry?'

'Yair,' replied Lester. 'Like everyone else.'

The sun touched the far horizon over which the flood water had raced to create Lake Otway. The galahs and the white cockatoos came seeking the water and found it, whirling down to settle on the flats either side the Channel.

Birds that had been watering every evening for three years at Lake Otway now came to the Channel. They alighted on the flats either side the thin ribbon of water, made suspicious at first by the fence and traps, massing in great patches of colours. The galahs crowded together their grey backs and the dots of pink combs, and the Major Mitchell cockatoos splashed white and raised their combs to produce pink dots on white.

They topped every inch of the fence and the trap-yards and tumbled to the verge of the water and lowered and lifted their heads like mechanical toys. Every minute additional flocks arrived. The crows came to whirl among those aloft and deliberately generate deeper suspicion in the vociferous parrots, and make still more shy the hundreds of emus who stalked the flats wide out.

'Better have a go for Gillen in the morning,' suggested MacLennon, his voice raised to defeat the cacophony of the birds. 'When d'you reckon Martyr ought to be back?'

'Some time tonight, if the Boss doesn't want him to go on

to the River,' replied Carney. 'Better hunt for Gillen in the morning, because after the Boss and the rest get out we won't stand a chance. It seems to be a matter of pulling together . . . or else.'

'Should have looked for him today,' Lester said.

'You seem mighty anxious, Bob,' sneered the ex-fighter.

'Yair,' agreed Lester with ill-feigned nonchalance. 'Seems we all got a stake in Gillen. Even me and George and Bony.'

'Meaning?' demanded MacLennon.

'You don't need tellin', Mac. Gillen had a lot of dough. He had a locket. The locket leads to the dough, don't it?'

'What the hell are you talking about?' asked Carney.

Lester actually giggled before he sniffled.

'Not much gets past me,' he claimed, triumph pictured on his unshaven face. 'Caw! Look at them birds.'

MacLennon wriggled sideways like a crab to bring himself closer and able to talk with less demand on his vocal chords. His broad features were distorted by anger.

'That locket belongs to me,' he shouted. 'I won it off Gillen, see? What's mine is mine. So you keep out of it, Bob. I'm meanin' that.'

'Quite a few birds around, eh?' remarked Carney to Bony, obviously with the intention of easing the strain. Of these three men, his was the firmest character and he was now beginning to assert it.

The appearance of Barby and Joan Fowler could have been the cause of MacLennon's withdrawal from argument. The trapper carried a bucket of hot coffee and the girl had brought a loaded dish of sweet scones. Wearing a pair of light drill trousers and a man's shirt, her almost blatant femininity was a travesty despite her powdered face and scarlet lips.

The first rabbit appeared to their right, running over the sandbar, running fast and direct, never pausing to look for possible enemies, flogged by the craving for water after the hours of terrible heat. The fence stopped it, flung it back, and it crouched obviously not understanding what had barred its progress.

The animal was recognizable only by its colour and shape, all its natural attributes of caution, of swift alertness, of gentle and graceful movement having vanished during the hours of its torture by the sun. It pawed the netting, frantically, standing on its hind legs, and not having the sense to climb the netting like a cat. It tested the wire with its teeth before running along the fence, to reach at last an inward pointing V, and so finding the hole to pass through. It thrust indignant birds aside to lap the water.

Carney touched Bony's arm and pointed over the depression.

'Fence won't stand up long after dark,' he worried.

Beyond the birds the kangaroos were gathering. The nearest were squatting, erect, ears attuned to catch the sounds about the trap, nostrils twitching to register suspicious scents. Beyond them others came loping over the dry lake bed, and already the dust rose from their passage.

The birds maintained their uproar, filling the air about the men. Birds were drowned in the Channel. Birds were staggering about on the marge inside the fence, their feathers wet, shieking anger and defiance, being buffeted by others and by rabbits.

There were now a dozen rabbits drinking. There were a hundred outside. They came like speeding drops of brown water over the dunes, over the flats, never halting, minus caution, motivated only by the urge to drink. They joined those at the fence, trickled through the holes to the water where they parted the birds to drink. The men watched the first water-laden rabbit enter a trap-yard.

An eagle appeared floating through the bird cloud. It tipped a wing and side-slipped to snatch a running rabbit. The rabbit hung by its rump from the iron beak, and they could see its pink mouth widen in a scream when, to stop its struggles, and to clear the lesser birds, the eagle drove its talons into its vitals. Through the birds on the flats, like a ship moving at sea, a dingo loped, betraying exhaustion, its red tongue lolling, its flanks tucked to its backbone. The dog took no notice of the rabbits or they of it. It butted the fence as though it were blind, sat and stared. The lolling tongue was drawn up under the snarling upper lip, and with the resolution of despair the animal drove at the netting, rose on hind legs to paw its way up and over. It plunged into the water and drank as it swam.

'I better fetch the guns,' Barby shouted.

'Bring mine, George!' requested MacLennon. 'And that red

box of cartridges on top of me swag. We gotta keep them 'roos off, or they'll flatten the fence.'

Lester went with George, and Bony glanced at the girl sitting with her hands clasped across her drawn-up knees. Her eyes were hooded. The evening light tended to soften her features, to give her hair a more brilliant tint. Carney moved to sit close to her, but she did not speak in answer to what he said, did not permit the intrusion to disturb her evident absorption in the terrible struggle for survival.

Bony went down to the fence where the rabbits were beginning to mass in a wide ribbon. They were pouring through the V points. They were jammed against the wire. They were gnawing at it, and none took notice of Bony's boots as he edged through them. A V point was choked by a rabbit that had died in the act of passing through, and he cleared the hole. He straightened the netting where the dingo had pawed it, and he witnessed the dog clamber over the opposite fence and lope slowly away.

The dusk was creeping over the depression, but the birds would not leave. They whirled about him like coloured snowflakes, and continued to cover the flats, and when he walked wide of the fence they reminded him of that evening Witlow and he had waded in Lake Otway and the ducks had parted before them and closed in after them.

On coming to the far end of the Channel he paused awhile to marvel at the number of kangaroos and to note that of all the animals they only still retained their normal attributes, and he was wondering if this was due to higher intelligence when his attention was caught by what could be the body of a large fish now beneath the coverlet of massed galahs. Had not the light been tricky, he might not have noticed this hump where one ought not to be.

Recalling Lester's theory of what had happened to Gillen's body, he walked on through the birds, who at this moment chose to rise with a roar of wings and screams of defiance and depart for roosts. Even when fifty yards off the hump he could not now see it, but eventually coming to it his curiosity was richly rewarded.

The skeleton was shrouded with tiny weeds which covered the floor of once Lake Otway, the weed now dead and brittle as it lay over the depression . . . a perfect camouflage.

He turned and slowly walked back to the Channel.

The 'roos crept after him. The rabbits came running between them, running after Bony, passing him, to run onward to the magnet of water. Without trouble, he caught one. It screamed and struggled. He put it down, and it ran on as though it had not been hindered.

Well, there was the unfortunate Gillen, and there were the men and the woman on the distant sandbar who had waited long for Lake Otway to die that they might find his remains. According to Lester, what the others wanted was the locket about the skeleton's neck, the locket giving the clue to Gillen's money. But Gillen's money was under Lester's bed. And Mrs Fowler was dead under the ruins of the homestead.

Again skirting the Channel, the last of the birds continued their struggle for water. Scores were drowned, others were drowning. The bodies of rabbits floated on the black surface. There were more living rabbits inside the fence than could find space at the water's edge, and now and then one of the drinkers was bitten and it leaped forward to plunge into the water and swim. They swam like dogs. All headed away from the land as though strongly determined to reach the other side, but in every case when they had proceeded a yard or two they panicked and swam in an ever-narrowing circle until they lowered their heads below the surface as though compelled to suicide.

The traps were deep with animals. At each corner they were standing on hind legs, biting the wire to get out, and, like little chickens who crowd into a corner and smother, so did the rabbits.

The party on the sandbar was breaking up, and Barby came hurrying to Bony, offering a Winchester rifle and a box of cartridges. The excitement in the trapper's eyes, the tremor in his voice, did not escape Bony or estrange his sympathy, for Barby was like a man who has stumbled on an outcrop of gold-loaded quartz.

'Goin' to be big, Bony,' he cried. 'I never knew it could be like this, did you?'

'No, George not like this,' Bony admitted. 'I'll go back to the tip of the Channel. Be sure to make the others understand where everyone is positioned, for when the moon goes down it will be very dark, and accidents can easily happen.'

'Yair. Right! I'll tell them. No firing at the fence, or along it, either. Thanks for giving a hand.'

Bony made his way back to the extremity of the Channel . . . made his way because he had literally to kick the rabbits from his path. The dusk was eating the salmon-pink dunes and the eagles were compelled at last to seek roosts on the topmost limbs of dead gums . . . that is, if they roosted at all, which Bony, like many bushmen, doubted.

He waved his gun and shouted, and the Channel behind him was now itself a living thing. It actually appeared to breathe, to pulsate, to moan and heave. Rabbits brushed against his legs. Rabbits sped over his feet. Rabbits surged over the now invisible ground like ocean waves on shingle.

Although he hated it, he had to do his share of defending the fence. He shot a kangaroo that rose up within two yards of him, and thereafter shot many others, taking small comfort in that the slaughter would provide Barby with hides for his market.

All about the Channel the foxes were gathering and barking as though in sadistic approval of this flameless hell.

20

The Skinners' Reward

It was almost dark before the birds ultimately gave up and retired. The guns barked spasmodically, and the crescent moon gave sufficient illumination to see creeping 'roos when but a few yards from the defenders. Had not thirst subdued caution the defenders might have won the battle: but what is to be done with a kangaroo who, taller than a man and twice his weight, bumps him aside like a woman determined to reach a bargain counter?

Barby came along the fence, chanting a lurid parody to give warning of his approach. Bony struck a match and, before the light expired, the trapper found him and sat with him on the ground.

'Keep 'em off for an hour if we can,' he said. 'How you going?'

'So far so good,' replied Bony. 'There will be quite a few 'roos around before midnight. Look at this gentleman.'

Bony struck another match and they found themselves confronted by an unusually large animal resting on its short forepaws and staring at them from what appeared to be the base of the small mountain of its hindquarters.

'Caw!' muttered Barby, and fired. 'Funny the noise of the guns and yelling and screaming don't have any effect, ain't it? Y'know, if I told me relations in England about this they'd call me a bloody liar to me face. Even if I had a camera and flash-bulbs they wouldn't believe the pictures. If only we had a movie camera. The chaps are going to look for Gillen at daybreak.'

'Oh! No skinning, then?'

'Me and the rabbits can go to hell. Even the cook's goin' to hunt for Gillen soon's it's light.'

'Joan?'

'Yair. Carney was trying to get the others to search by a plan, but it looks like they'll keep together for fear one finds and the others miss out.'

To all points, far and near, the foxes barked. The moon hung low across the depression, and now and then it was temporarily eclipsed by a moving animal.

'Let them hunt, George. I'll give a hand with the skinning.'

'Thanks, Bony, old feller. They won't find him. Gillen's down on the bottom of the Channel, and by morning there'll be a ton or two of dead rabbits on top of him. We'll keep our eyes on 'em, all the same. I'll make me way back to see to the V holes. Must keep 'em clear. I'll shout and bawl when we knocks off and lifts the netting to let the mob in for a drink. They'll be back tomorrow night.'

Barby left, and shortly afterwards a fox came close. Bony heard its panting, and then felt its breath strike against his face. He thrust the rifle forward and the muzzle encountered the fox, who snapped at the steel. Hastily Bony stood. Better to have an ankle bitten than his face or an arm.

It was only a few minutes after nine, when he heard Barby

shouting and the men answering and he proceeded to roll the netting up from the ground and sling it from the top of the stakes. Every step he took he trod on rabbits. They surged about his feet like strips of blanket energized with power. Then the netting ahead of him jerked under his hand and he knew, although he could not see, that a kangaroo was entangled in it.

Lights appeared in the direction of the sandbar, and someone carried a lamp along the fence to him. It was Carney, and Carney took his rifle to allow him to use both hands.

'Martyr should be here. Write a poem about it,' commented Carney. 'The place is going to look sort of peculiar in the morning.'

'Probably just one big heap of rotting fur,' Bony predicted.

The light revealed a scene of such prodigious struggle for survival that both men were awed. A huge kangaroo squatted at the water and drank, flanked by a seething mass of rabbits, Gulliver crowded by the Lilliputians. A fox stood drinking with the rabbits under its belly, with a rabbit crouched between its forepaws and lapping the water. Another 'roo appeared, moving like a spider, flinging rabbits out of its path, its muzzle stretched forward as though the head was impatient of the lethargic body. It ranged alongside the fox, which continued imbibing. A half-bred dingo appeared in the radius of the lamplight, and it seemed to run on rabbits to reach the water it lapped and lapped as though determined never to stop.

Then men moved along the fence lifting the netting, before them a carpet of frantic animals trying to reach water, and after them a violent mêlée. Bony saw a 'roo turn from the water and accidentally swipe a fox with its tail. The fox was knocked into the water, and it continued to drink even as it swam.

'Aw, let the netting stop,' Carney urged when another kangaroo was entangled with the roll they had left suspended on the stakes. 'There'll be no fence in the morning, and the netting will never be fit for anything again.'

'I think you're right,' Bony agreed, but they went on with the task till they were met by Lester on the same work.

'Cripes! You oughta see what's in the traps,' he chortled. 'Four million rabbits in each of 'em.'

'Have you counted them?' Bony inquired, and wished he hadn't, for the question brought the sniffle.

'No. I give up when I got to ten thousand.'

They came to a trap-yard. The interior was a block of animals, only those on top of the mass being alive.

Barby came, saying dolefully:

'What a ruddy mess! Stonker the crows! You blokes will have to lend a hand in the morning. Money! Money! Money! Come on! Let's eat.'

On the sandbar, Bony paused to listen. Mercifully hidden by the night, the titanic struggle for life-saving water created sound which could be likened by the imaginative to the snoring of a prehistoric beast, and that sound dwindled as Bony passed on beyond the sandbar, dwindled till he could no longer hear it, and was glad. But memory retained a picture of the green and the red lights which had ringed them as they lifted the netting ... the lamp-light reflected by the eyes of tortured animals.

Later, when they had washed and eaten and drunk enormous quantities of sugarless coffee, Barby brought up the subject of skinning his 'catch'.

'We'll get on with that later,' insisted MacLennon, and Lester sniffled and said:

'Yair. After we've found Gillen and the locket.'

'You remember what happened to you when you'd dug out them Paddy's ducks,' snarled MacLennon. 'That locket's mine. And no bloody arguing.'

'Oh no it's not,' Joan exclaimed, and, being near MacLennon, turned to smile contemptuously at him.

Bony spoke coolly:

'Where do you expect to find the remains of Gillen?' Everyone turned to him, everyone save Barby.

'On the Lake somewhere or other,' replied MacLennon. 'You keep out, anyhow. Nothin' to do with you.'

'Perhaps not,' conceded Bony. 'On the other hand perhaps you would like to be saved much walkabout in the heat tomorrow.'

They crowded him. He looked at them in turn, their faces clearly revealed by the leaping firelight.

'Well, what's to it?' demanded Carney.

'Merely that you should walk in circles and never find the

remains of Ray Gillen. I will lead you, all of you, to the remains in the morning. After.'

'After! What d'you mean, after?' Lester asked.

'After we have skinned the rabbits in George's two traps.'

'Strike me flamin' blue!' exploded MacLennon. 'What a hope.'

'Good on you, Bony,' chortled Barby, and Bony said:

'Fair's fair. You help to skin the rabbits, and I take you to Gillen's body. You don't skin the rabbits, and you promenade in the gentle heat of western New South Wales. It's all yours, dear brethren.'

The girl confronted Bony, mouth uplifted, eyes blue-green like opals.

'Truly, you know where he is?' she asked, admiringly.

'I know where the body is, as I told you. When the rabbits are skinned, I'll take all of you to the place. Quite simple.'

The smile settled about her mouth, and on her turning to the men her voice contained an underlying note of steel. 'You heard what Bony said, Harry, Mac and Bob. That's final. You'll skin the damn rabbits. We'll all go with Bony in the morning . . . and don't try to be clever.'

'Suits me,' agreed Carney.

'Me, too,' added Lester, and Bony silently complimented him.

Thereafter a truce settled on them and the subject of Gillen and his locket was not mentioned. For a while they squatted or sat inside the circle of firelight, and all agreed when Carney said that Martyr must have gone on to the main homestead after telephoning from Sandy Creek.

'No one will get here till about eleven tomorrow,' Lester estimated. 'That'll give us time to skin them blasted rabbits for George and then Bony will do what he promised.'

Half an hour later, Carney announced his intention of having some 'shut-eye', and the girl rose, saying she needed sleep if no one else did. And yet they waited for Bony.

Bony brought his swag and unrolled it in the firelight. He undressed only by removing his boots. Lester brought his swag and laid it on the ground nearby, and MacLennon and Carney did likewise. They were not going to lose Bony to any artful dodger, and he was highly amused when the girl staggered from behind the hut, carrying the bedding so carefully arranged for her.

To see them composed for sleeping within a few feet of the camp fire, it would be difficult to believe that the temperature of the night was above the century.

When the sky proclaimed the coming of the day, Barby had the coffee bubbling and was frying flapjacks and grilling kangaroo steaks, and before it was possible to read a newspaper away from the firelight, they trudged over the sandbar armed with skinning knives and bags to take the rabbit skins.

The Channel wasn't to be seen. It was marked by the sturdy corner posts of the two trap-yards, and a few of the fence stakes. The rolled netting appeared here and there above the dun-coloured mass which covered the ground and stiffened the surface of the water invisible beneath the bodies of the drowned. Back from this dreadful immobility, the living were dazed like zombies. Kangaroos were gouging among the dead with their paws, thrusting their muzzles among the dead to make space to get at the water. Hundreds were sitting up at varying distances, with rabbits moving among them, and among the rabbits the foxes were walking with grotesque daintiness.

The men skinned diligently, and Bony noted their reaction to this work. The girl mystified him, for she watched the skinners and now and then regarded the background of their work with undoubted enjoyment. MacLennon was sullen; Carney was, as usual, cheerful; Lester worked fast and automatically, because his mind wasn't on the job.

Some of the kangaroos returned ... those who hadn't reached the water. The rabbits were gathering into heaps about the dead 'roos, and these were doomed as they had not taken in water and instincts were shattered. Now and then a flock of birds came to whirl above the Channel and depart at high speed as though aware they must find water before the sun again became a killer. The crows attacked the living rodents gathered in growing heaps, for when a rabbit died others crowded on it, too stupefied to run for cover from the risen sun.

'Righto, blokes, no more,' Barby called. 'The sun's rotting 'em already. We musta got through four thousand.'

The fur was gathered into bags to keep till dried on the wire bows. Thousands of carcasses were left in the one trap-yard: the other wasn't touched and now the sun was destroying hundreds of pounds worth of fur. MacLennon said:

'It's up to you, Bony. We got to go far?'

'No. You understand, I hope, that if you interfere with the remains the police will be annoyed?'

'My troubles!' snorted MacLennon.

'And that the locket, if still with the body, is the property of the State?'

'Just too bad,' sneered Lester. 'Caw! You talk like a judge.'

They proceeded, the four men and the girl keeping close to Bony.

'I don't understand your avid interest in a locket you claim was worn by Gillen when he was drowned,' he said. 'I'm not going to be drawn into any trouble with you or the police. If, as I said, you interfere with the remains, the police will want to know why. They would say that until the authorities prove Gillen was drowned, it could be that one of you murdered him. They will certainly want that locket. Why is it so important to all of you? What d'you want the locket for?'

'Just to see what's inside it,' replied Lester.

'You ain't got no right . . . ' MacLennon began, when Carney stopped him.

'Now look, Mac, let's recognize facts, and let's behave decently. It wouldn't get us anywhere if we all rushed it like a pack of dingoes. We'll let Bony find the locket, and we'll let him open it for us all to see.'

'Fair enough,' agreed Lester, but MacLennon started again to argue, and this time Joan stopped him with a verbal lashing which stunned Bony and caused Lester to sniffle thrice.

They did not see the weed-shrouded remains of Raymond Gillen until Bony stopped and indicated the skeleton. Silently he waited, and one by one they looked up and into his wide and ice-blue eyes.

Carney was grave and self-possessed. Lester licked his upper lip, and the watery blue eyes were avaricious. The girl's mouth was compressed to a straight thin line of scarlet. Barby was white about the nostrils, and MacLennon's face was twitching at the corners of his mouth and under his cheek-bones.

'Go on, Bony, get it,' cried Joan.

'All right! Now stand away, all of you.' They drew back,

and he ordered them to retire still farther. They obeyed. He sank to his knees, continuing to watch them. He delved with his hand under the skeleton. The cord had vanished. A little groping, and he found the key. The locket was half-buried in the sludge. He stood, showing the locket to the watchers, and they surged forward to surround him. Carney exclaimed:

'Good on you, Bony! Open it for us.'

21

The Locket

UNHURRIEDLY, BONY rubbed the locket against his trousers to clean it of weed and dried mud. The four men watched his hand manipulating the locket; the girl watched his eyes, enigmatically. He was smiling. A lesser man might have so reacted to this situation creating self-importance, but to Bony it was merely the prelude.

MacLennon twisted his great hands about each other; intent like an eagle ready to pounce. Carney stood with hands against his hips, balanced on his toes, an easy smile about his mouth and faint amusement in his eyes. Lester forbore to sniffle. His mouth was slightly open, and for once his eyes were strong and steady. George Barby's teeth were worrying his upper lip. There was a vertical frown between his brows, and perplexity was clearly defined. For a long second Bony's eyes clashed with the girl's green eyes, suddenly wide and probing.

The locket was heart-shaped, of modern design and was studded with a solitary square-cut sapphire. When Bony displayed it on the palm of his hand, the others crowded about him.

He was unable to open it with a thumb-nail, and Barby presented a clasp-knife. Deliberately, he prised the locket apart on its hinges, to reveal on the one side the picture of a woman and on the other that of a man.

Suspended breathing hissed from MacLennon, and Lester sniffled and deserved a cuff.

'Get the pictures out, Bony,' urged Carney. 'Could be writing on the back.'

With slight difficulty, Bony managed to lift out the picture of the woman. There was writing on the back of the print ... the word 'Mum'. On the reverse of the picture of the man was the word 'Pop'.

'There doesn't seem to be anything else,' drawled Bony.

'Lemme look,' rasped MacLennon, and Carney said, warningly:

'Go easy, Mac. Look again, Bony. Look for small letters scratched outside or inside the locket. There's something we want to see.'

'There is nothing,' Bony said after a swift examination of the locket. 'What did you expect to see?'

MacLennon cursed and grabbed, but Bony's fingers imprisoned the locket. He stepped back to avoid MacLennon's punch and then Joan was confronting the ex-pugilist and shouting:

'You animal, Mac! Behave yourself.'

'It's my locket, Joan. It's mine.'

'Shut up,' cried the girl furiously. 'It's mine more than yours.' She swung about to confront Barby. 'You look at it, George. Bony can't see anything. I can't see anything, and Mac can't, either. But you look at it to satisfy him.'

'Damned if I know what all the botheration is about,' Barby said, flatly. 'There's nothing inside the locket bar the two pictures, and there's nothing on the back of them except "Mum" and "Pop". Why the fuss?'

'Gillen had a lot of money, that's why,' bawled MacLennon, surging past Joan.

Joan opened her mouth, caught back the words. Carney grinned, and this abused word is the correct one to describe his expression. Lester licked his drooping moustache like a dingo watching a fox being killed by eagles. Still perplexed, the trapper said:

'Gillen had money, so what? Did one of you murder him for it?'

They became still, and passivity was smashed by MacLennon.

'He could of been, George,' he shouted. 'I wouldn't know. He had a lot of money in his case, wads and wads of it. Must have stolen it from a bank or something. He woke up to someone after it, and planted it and put the clue to the place in the locket. We been waiting for the tide to go down to get at that locket . . . all of us.'

'Not me,' chirped Lester. 'I knew nothing about no locket.'

'Lot of rot, seems to me,' drawled Carney, rocking on his heels. 'Better quit and pass it up.'

'No damn fear,' roared the heavy man. 'Someone's got Gillen's dough. And I'm having me share, or else.'

'Me, too,' interjected Lester. 'Find anything, George?'

'Nothing,' replied Barby, and slipped the pictures into place and closed the locket.

'But there is. There must be. Gillen said there was,' persisted the enraged MacLennon.

'All right, Mac. You look.'

MacLennon snatched the locket and opened it easily with his thumb-nail. He dug the pictures out with his dirty nail, peered at them with screwed-up eyes, and at the locket inside and out. And with varying reactions the others waited, united only in contempt for this Doubting Thomas. Bony stood a little to the rear of the group, his fingers working at a cigarette but his eyes missing nothing. He hoped for more from MacLennon, and was given more. The big man threw locket and pictures to the ground and with hands knotted into clubs glared at them.

'One of you got here first. You got here 'fore we did, Bony.'

The limelight played on Bony, and Bony nodded.

'Yes, just before dark last night. You asked me to get the locket for you if I should find the remains. Joan did, too. But the locket belongs to the State, who will hold it for the rightful owner at law. The State is going to ask us a lot of questions, such as how did the locket come to be forced open and the pictures tossed on the ground. And what is this yarn about a lot of money in a dead man's suitcase. In fact, the State is going to be most tiresome.'

'I told you to shut up, you fool,' snarled the girl at MacLennon. 'Harry tried to shut you up, too. Now spit out the rest of it and be a bigger fool.'

'All right, I will,' roared MacLennon. 'Harry showed us a letter writ by Gillen, saying he'd spotted his case being interfered with, and that he'd planted his money and put the clue to the place inside his locket. So if the one who mucked about with his case really wanted his dough he'd know where to find the clue but they'd have to get the locket off him first. Twelve thousand quid and some was what Gillen had, according to you, Joan. You told us Gillen had showed you that dough to make himself sweet with you. And Harry found the letter in the case instead of the money . . . accordin' to him.'

'Could of been some double-crossing,' followed Lester's sniffle.

'Yair, of course,' shouted MacLennon. 'One of you got in first. One of you got that money. And by hell I'm gettin' my share of it. I'll . . . smash your rotten . . .'

'You'll drop in a fit, that's what you'll be doing,' sneered the girl.

She received a slap to the face which sent her backwards. Carney sprang at MacLennon and got in a right royal haymaker which splayed the ex-pugilist. Then they went to it, and Carney quickly proved he was no gentleman in a real Australian brawl . . . boots and all.

The girl scrambled to her feet. Lester danced and sniffled and shouted:

'Four to one, Carney! Sock it in, Harry. Four to one Mother's boy. Let 'em alone, Joan! Get off it! Cripes! Odds is short now. Two to one, Carney. Caw! Let 'em alone!'

Joan was hanging to the big man's shirt and kicking at his ankles. Carney got in a walloper, and Lester began the count. Calmly, without the trace of a smile, George Barby remarked to Bony:

'When thieves fall out, honest men like you and me steps in.'

Bony was reminded of a picture of hounds pulling down a stag. He retrieved the locket and the miniatures, replaced the pictures, and pocketed the locket. Then he smiled at Barby:

'It must be time for smoko, George.'

'Yair. Very dry argument this morning, Bony.'

Carney was kneeling and waving his hands as though in obeisance to King Sol. Joan was behind MacLennon and doing her utmost to scalp him. MacLennon was yelling, and Lester was urging Joan to 'pull his ears off'. Then Carney left the ground in a flying tackle and the combatants became a heap. Bony turned away, and Barby walked at his side and said:

'Did you hear Ray Gillen laughing and laughing?'

'Yes, I heard it,' Bony replied, gravely. 'I thought it was ghostly merriment.'

They came to the Channel, invisible beneath the covering of drowned animals. The crows were now the flakes of a black snowstorm, and dotted on the flats the eagles were gorging. Here and there, farther away, daintily walked the emus, their tail feathers billowing like the skirts of a ballerina. The kangaroos had gone, but a few of the galah host still lingered about the dunes.

'Funny about that letter MacLennon said Carney found in Gillen's suitcase,' Barby drawled. 'What d'you make of it?'

'I wish that MacLennon had been a little more elucidative, George. It does seem that Carney found such a letter in Gillen's case, and we may assume that Carney found that letter after Gillen went swimming, that he was anxious about the money, having been told by Joan how much there was, Joan having been told by Gillen. Which supports what you overheard that night when Joan and Carney discussed money. We now know why no one left Lake Otway after Gillen was drowned. Why everyone was so interested in Lake Otway's inevitable demise. Did you ever see Gillen writing letters?'

'Can't say I ever did,' replied Barby, taking up one of the bags containing rabbit pelts. 'Never said anything about his mother or father, or about any pals.'

Bony heaved a bag to his back, and together they went on. Near the sandbar, Bony turned to see the three battlers and the referee walking slowly after them. They were widely spaced, and obviously not engaged in friendly conversation.

'It is going to be abnormally hot today,' he told Barby. 'I wonder what has happened to Martyr. Someone ought to have arrived by now. Must be after nine o'clock.'

'Ought to come any time. I'm goin' to get on with stretchin' these skins. Won't have a chance after the mob gets here. Betcher the Sergeant'll be out askin' questions. What do we say about the locket?'

'Haven't decided. I think the police will be far too interested in the fire and the fate of Mrs Fowler to bother about Gillen's remains just now. Have you enough bows for all these pelts?'

'Not near enough.'

'Then I'll cut some more after smoko.'

They dumped the heavy loads in tree shadow. The dogs welcomed them dispiritedly. The cats yawned and went to sleep again. The pet galah screeched, and Barby opened its cage door and it fell over itself, such was its haste to gain freedom. A rabbit had found a bread-crust at the edge of ash marking the fire site . . . and continued to eat.

Bony took empty water-buckets to the reservoir tank, and saw rabbits crouching under the long trough. The trough was empty and he removed the chock from under the ball valve and permitted water to gush into it. Immediately, crows appeared to caw raucously, and galahs came to perch on the trough edges. Barby's dogs jumped into the water and lapped as it ran under their tummies. The rabbits beneath the trough waited for the water to drip from the iron seams.

The warriors entered camp, Carney carrying the third bag of skins. They were sullenly silent, and the men stripped to the waist and carried towels to the trough to bathe their bruises and abrasions. On his way with filled buckets, Bony encountered Joan, whose left cheek was still inflamed by the smack from MacLennon. She actually smiled at him, but it didn't raise his blood pressure.

In sullen silence a meal was eaten, and afterwards Bony took a file to a heap of old fencing wire and cut lengths to be bent to U shape. Lester assisted Barby to stretch the pelts over the bows and thrust them upright by pushing the points into the soft ground. The skins were board-hard and dry in less than twenty minutes, and eventually were removed and packed into a wool-sack.

When it was ten o'clock, the heat was almost combustible. Lester estimated the temperature to be about 112 degrees; Carney 115 degrees. The cats demanded watered tummies, and the galah sought similar attention from the solicitous Barby. Immediately the tea-billy was empty, another was placed on the fire, smokeless and almost invisible in the glare of the sun.

The men and the girl clung to the shadow cast by the hut. Whenever they drank, perspiration oozed from face and body within minutes. Joan had a basin of water and she saturated somebody's shirt and draped it about her head. Carney wished they had a pack of cards.

It was just before eleven, and Lester was voicing doubt

that Martyr could have reached the telephone at Sandy Well, when the crow fell from the cabbage tree where Bony had tethered his horse. It uttered a long-drawn c-a-a-h as it nose-dived to the ground without a flutter

'Last time I seen anything like that,' Lester said, 'the local shade temperature was 123 degrees.'

'That's what it is here and now,' Carney stated with conviction.

'Assuming that Martyr's utility broke down between Lake Otway and Sandy Well, what would he do?' Bony asked, and Carney answered him.

'He'd try and fix the trouble. He had a full gallon water-bag for himself, and a tinful for the radiator. And a mile off the track midway there's a well called The Shaft. If he couldn't get the lump of junk to go, he'd wait till night and walk on to Sandy Well.'

'And if he didn't get to Sandy Well by nine last night, more'n likely there'd be no one in the River office to answer his ringing,' supplemented Barby. 'That would mean he'd camp there and wait for the Boss to ring at half-past seven this morning.'

'What do you think Wallace would do on being told about the fire?' persisted Bony, actually to break up a moody silence.

'He'd tell Martyr he'd be out as soon as he could. He'd know we was all right, and Martyr was all right,' replied Barby. 'Mr Wallace would ring the police at Menindee, and the Sergeant would have to get a doctor, and as far as I know the nearest doctor would be at Broken Hill, seventy miles off. Or he might come out without a doctor. I reckon Wallace would come out without waiting for the Sergeant.'

'What good would a doctor do? Tell us that,' sharply urged Joan.

'A doctor has to certify how your mother died,' Bony said, adding: 'And also how Gillen died.'

22

Something to do

AFTER DAYS AND nights when the air had remained still, the wind came. It was neither strong nor gusty: a gentle wind in pressure, but hated for its heat. It came from over the depression, came over the sandbar and down along the creek bed to destroy even the imaginary coolness of the shadows. It lacked even the virtue of strength sufficient to worry the flies.

They could escape the flies by entering the hut, but the interior of the hut wasn't to be borne longer than a few seconds. Two could have gone down the well and stood on the platform supporting the pump seventy feet underground. There the temperature was about sixty degrees, but the cramped position would be too much and the climb down and up the ladder fastened to the wall of the shaft not lightly to be undertaken by the allegedly weakest of the party, Joan Fowler.

Barby plunged an old cooking apron into a water-bucket, and with this about his head and shoulders he took the bucket to refill. There were no birds attempting to drink the water in the trough; there wasn't a bird on the wing. The water in the trough was hot.

While filling his bucket from the tank, Barby heard the crows in the tree from which one had fallen dead, and threw an old jam tin among the branches. Several crows flew from the close-set foliage, loudly complaining, and before they had proceeded a dozen yards from the shelter they turned and almost fell back into it.

'Hot water on tap,' Barby said on his return to the hut shade. 'See them crows? They'll put on a turn soon, believe you me.'

Bony alone appeared interested.

Barby set down the bucket and the galah fell into the hole made for it before water could be poured into the hole. The cats didn't move, and he poured water on them. They refrained from licking the water from their fur. One of the dogs looked as though about to die, and he procured a pair of hair clippers and proceeded to shear it, for something to do.

'Hell of a long time since she was as hot as this,' Lester said. 'Must be over 120 degrees in this shade, anyhow. The old man usta tell of a heat-wave they had when he run the pub. It was so hot all you had to do to light a match was to hold it in the sun for a sec.'

Carney extracted a wax vesta from a box and tossed it from the shadow. He lay watching it for some time before saying:

'Not as hot as your old man's pub, Bob. I say, George, what about taking a run to the homestead in the ute? Something to do to pass the time.'

'Too hot to shift the ute,' Barby objected. 'Besides, we'd go less than a mile when her petrol would be all gas and she'd stop dead. I'm staying right here. Look! Your match is burnt.'

'You'd be right ... about the petrol turning to gas,' Carney agreed. 'That's it! That's why no one has come from the River. Car's stuck up on the track somewhere. Hell, they'll be hot if they are.'

He tossed another match to fall on the shadeless ground and waited for it to ignite. A second crow fell from the tree, but he didn't remove his gaze from the match.

Something to do was becoming a powerful need, even for Bony. Merely to sit and wait was, psychologically, to add another ten degrees to the temperature. He draped his shirt over his head and shoulders and went for a bucket of water. That was something to do and he felt better even though the short journey back with the filled bucket made him feel slightly giddy.

The gentle wind direct from an imagined furnace continued. It softly rustled the leaves of the cabbage tree. It sent the sap from all the tree branches down the trunks to the roots, and branches weakened by termites or dry rot began to crash to the ground. Bony saw one branch fall, and heard others fall from distant trees along the creek. To Carney he said:

'Supposing that Martyr's utility held him up and he was

unable to reach Sandy Well, what would have happened at the River homestead?'

'Well, the Boss would have tried to raise the out-station last night at seven as usual,' Carney replied, having waited for the sun to fire his second match. 'Not being able to raise anyone he might get the cook at Sandy Well to have a go. Then he'd decide that the telephone at the out-station must be out of order, and he'd know Martyr had a spare one and would ring through sometime. This morning when the Boss rang through at half-past seven, and got nothing, he'd reckon the line was down between here and Sandy Well.'

'And knowing nothing about the fire, and there being nothing important to discuss, the Boss would patiently wait?'

'Yair. Wait on the cool homestead veranda, while one of his daughters supplied him with iced gin slings.'

'Has the cook, or anyone at Sandy Well, a motor vehicle?'

'No. If Martyr don't contact him by this evening, the Boss might get one of the riders at the Well to follow the line out from here. And if no one turns up here by nine tonight, I reckon something serious has happened to Martyr.'

'I am beginning to think that,' admitted Bony. He glanced at MacLennon, who was lying on his back and hadn't spoken for more than an hour. The girl was sitting against the hut wall, her eyes closed, a spray of gum leaves serving her as a fly-whisk. Barby spoke:

'What we all want this warm day is a good feed of trebly-hot curry. I'm goin' to make one that'll turn your eyes back to front.'

Lester voted the curried tinned meat 'a corker'. Barby certainly put everything he had into it, but no persuasion would induce MacLennon to get up and eat.

'Let the hunk starve,' advised Joan, and when Lester was about to jibe, Barby restrained him.

Bony saw the white cockatoo drop dead from a near box tree, and he anticipated that, despite Barby's attention, the pet galah would not live the day through. The hot wind died away, but its departure gave no relief. What did bring relief, although of short duration, was the shouted declaration by MacLennon that he was 'going home'.

'To hell with the lot of you,' he told them when on his feet. 'I'm going home now.'

'Oh well, have a nice time,' drawled Carney.

The big man strode into the sunlight, and Bony called after him that he had forgotten his hat. MacLennon mightn't have heard, for he walked on, his over-long hair matted with sweat and dust.

'Come back for your hat, Mac,' shouted Barby, but the big man did not turn, did not halt, and they watched him pass over the sandbar and knew he intended following the flats.

'Ruddy idiot,' snorted Barby, and poured water over his cats.

Bony drenched a shirt with water and draped it about his head. He picked up MacLennon's hat and took down a water-bag from a wire hook.

'Let the fool go if he likes, Bony,' Joan urged.

'Yair,' supported Lester. 'He won't go far. Thirst'll hunt him back here.'

'It will be something to do,' Bony told them, and set off after MacLennon.

The sunlight burned his arms and 'bounced' off the red earth to hurt his eyes, but these discomforts were little to what he met when he passed over the sandbar to the depression.

The rank water in the Channel, its banks, the man-made traps and the wreckage of wire netting were a horrible picture which Bony tried to shun. Beyond the Channel, MacLennon was walking direct over the depression towards the distant out-station, and the mirage heightened his massive figure, making him a giant wading into the ocean.

Bony shouted but the man took no need. To run after him, even to hasten, would be to fall victim to the power from which he hoped to save MacLennon. As bad as the burning heat was the fierce light, which had no colour and contained an element of density, itself threatening to impede movement. His eyes shrank inward to the shade of the garment protecting his head, and for long moments he was compelled to keep the lids tightly lowered.

He did not see MacLennon struck by the sun, did not see him till about to pass him, and then MacLennon was groping on his hands and knees, and was blind and babbling.

'Get up and come back with me,' commanded Bony.

MacLennon did not hear. He was following a small circle,

and Bony was horribly reminded of the drowning rabbits. When Bony poured water from the bag upon the back of his head, neck and shoulders, he betrayed no reaction, and continued his unintelligible babbling.

Bony slapped a naked shoulder and shouted in an effort to make the man stand. Beyond this, common sense halted effort, for physical exertion beyond the minimum would bring collapse. He did think his urging was successful when MacLennon abruptly stood. He made five long strides, bringing the knees high and keeping his arms flung wide as though in balance. Then he crashed, falling on his face and lying still.

Bony knelt beside him and sheltered him with his own shadow. The warning to himself was unmistakable. The ground about the fallen man was magnified with such brilliance that the pin-points of rusty clay on a sliver of débris, the hairs on MacLennon's neck, even the nodules of dust on the man's back, appeared as large protuberances.

Despite the warning, Bony succeeded in turning MacLennon on his back . . . when death was evident.

During a long moment Bony fought for self-control. The bad moment passed, and his maternal ancestors crowded about him, whispering and cajoling. They pleaded with him to remain passive if only for a minute. They told him of their battle with this homicidal sun, brought to him their lore and wisdom. They implored him to drink and pour the remainder of the water on his head.

But the bag was empty.

Presently he felt a little better though vertigo remained a threat. He peered from the protection offered by the shirt to estmate distance to the sandbar. He found that the shore dunes were closer, and he could see a tea-tree bush growing between two dunes. It looked black against the red sand, and black spelled shade.

In the act of standing he remembered the crows, and couldn't leave MacLennon entirely to them, so he stepped from his trousers and made the garment a covering for his head: the shirt he laid over the dead face.

The ground heaved as he walked away from MacLennon. He fought back the impulse to run to the tea-tree shade, and slowly the bush grew in size, and slowly its shade came to meet him and became large enough to accept him.

He remembered he had once seen a thermometer at a homestead registering a point above 122 degrees, but that day the wind was blowing strongly. Today, here and now, there was no wind, not a current of air to be felt by the skin. The windless day is opportunity for the sun.

He was debating the subject of heat apoplexy, and the relation to it of perspiration, or lack of it, when he realized he could not remain in this shade without water. Already thickening saliva was swelling his tongue and gumming his lips.

He espied the nearest shade fifty yards towards the creek, a black ribbon lying over the ground cast by the trunk of a dead belar. Where the shadow joined the foot of the tree crouched a rabbit, and he did not see the rabbit until, struck by his foot, it fled into the sunlight. He watched it run to a steep sand dune, watched it scrambling upward and dislodging a minor avalanche. The animal was near the summit when it gave a convulsive leap, rolled down the slope and lay still.

'That was quicker than MacLennon got it,' he said, and knew he couldn't have been vocal.

Thus from shadow to shadow he accomplished the journey back to the creek trees, and, remembering the guest at Johnson's Well, he put on his trousers and crossed the creek with the empty water-bag on his head for protection.

They noted the absence of his shirt and MacLennon's hat.

'You caught up with the fool,' Lester stated as fact.

Bony nodded and sat with them in the hut shadow, now larger in area. There was a pannikin of warm tea beside Lester, and he 'sloshed' his mouth with the liquid because he couldn't part his lips.

'A bit generous, giving him your shirt,' snorted Barby, and again Bony nodded, now able to draw the liquid in between his lips and about the swollen tongue. Pride was digging into him. It would never do to permit these men and the girl to realize how soft he was, how close he'd come to meeting Sol's bolt. They were watching him closely, and with well-acted casualness he emptied the pannikin and borrowed Lester's tobacco and papers. Having made the cigarette, and having fought down the desire for more tea, he accepted a match from Carney.

'MacLennon didn't go far,' he said, and was inwardly pleased he was able to speak clearly. 'About half a mile on from the Channel.'

'What d'you mean?' asked the girl, impatiently.

'What he said,' Carney told her. 'Without a hat, and no shirt on, course he wouldn't get far.'

'Well, I hope he's dead,' Joan snapped, and, without looking at her, Bony related his adventure.

'And you left your shirt on him,' Barby said.

'I remembered the crows,' Bony told them, and the girl sneered.

'More fool you, Bony,' she jibed, and laughed.

23

Proceed as Usual

HOURS LATER, when the shadows were noticeably longer, Bony suggested that someone should accompany Barby to the out-station and, if no one was there, take the track to Sandy Well to locate Martyr and the main homestead. The suggestion found favour, and everyone wanted to go with Barby.

'All right! We'll all go. Better than sitting on our sterns. What's to be done about MacLennon?'

The question was put to Bony, and the others, waiting for his views, didn't realize how much his ego was boosted. Lester sniffled:

'Could do with a morgue, there's bodies all over the scenery.'

He was told by Carney to shut up, and Bony said:

'Because of the birds and the dingoes, the body should be put inside the hut. We could make a start now. While the body is being brought in, perhaps someone could bake something to go with George's tins of beef. We must take plenty of water in case we break down when trailing Martyr.'

It was arranged that Lester get on with baking scones, the girl would prepare another curry, and Bony would fill petrol tins with water. Carney went off with Barby in the utility. Eventually, the dogs having been fed, the cats attended to and the pet galah imprisoned in his cage, the party left Johnson's Well.

The sun was then a mighty crimson orb low over the depression, and it was setting when they arrived at the out-station. No voice hailed them, and Lester insisted on leaving the vehicle to look at the thermometer under the pepper trees.

'What next?' snarled Barby, but stopped none the less. 'Sun going down, getting a bit cool, and he wants to see if it's true.'

Lester jumped to the ground and slouched to the instrument. They saw him peering at it. He straightened and peered again. Then he shouted:

'A hundred and nineteen and a bit. Caw! Wonder it ain't busted.'

Forgetting to sniffle, he climbed on to the body of the ute.

'You sure?' demanded Carney.

'Take a deck yourself,' snapped Lester. 'A hundred and nineteen now. What must she have been round about two this afternoon? A flamin' record, I bet.'

They left the empty out-station, took the track up the long slope, and passed over the crest where Bony had observed the dust left by Martyr. No one looked back. Those on the tray body stood to look over the cabin top. They could see the track winding ahead for several miles. It was empty.

The normally red land, now covered by areas of dry grass dotted by clumps of belar and mulga, was apricot and silver in the waning evening light. They were grateful for the breeze created by the speed of the utility, and for the conquest of wind over flies.

Now and then Lester, clinging with Bony and Carney to the cabin top, sniffled and snortled.

'A hundred and nineteen at six o'clock!'

It was dark when they topped the following swell, and there Barby braked the vehicle to a stop, for far away blazed the lights of several vehicles coming their way. It being obviously unnecessary to go further, Barby turned the ute, cut his engine and climbed from the cabin.

'Three,' he said. 'Martyr in his ute, the Boss in his chromium chariot, and Red driving the juggernaut.'

'Hardly be Red, George, He wouldn't be able to keep up,' Carney pointed out.

'There's three coming, anyhow.'

'The third is probably being driven by a policeman,' offered Bony, and after that no one spoke.

Presently the lights caught them, and ultimately the first car stopped a few yards away. From the driver's window the overseer called:

'Righto, George! Get going back. I can give room here.'

The girl got in beside Martyr. Carney went with Barby, Lester seemed undecided, but followed Carney. Bony vanished. He reappeared beside Sergeant Mansell, who was driving the third vehicle.

'Been a hot day, Sergeant,' he remarked when climbing into the rear seat.

'Terrible,' replied the heavy man in plain clothes and, being uncertain of the identity Bony wished recognized for the benefit of the man sitting with him, added:

'A hundred and twenty-four at Menindee. One degree lower at Porchester homestead.'

'Must be a record, surely.'

'Easily. Broken Hill radio just said it's been 117 degrees down in Sydney. Dozens of people collapsed. Nearly did myself. Fires raging in Victoria. Doctor here wouldn't leave till four o'clock.'

'Too damned hot to move,' declared the doctor.

'You might introduce us, Sergeant.'

'Sure. Detective-Inspector Bonaparte . . . Doctor Clive.' The acknowledgements were given. 'How do we go,' Inspector?'

'As we were for the moment,' replied Bony. 'I am thankful you were able to come along, Doctor. There are three bodies to be dealt with: death by fire, assumed; death by drowning, assumed; and death by heat, easily established.'

'Quite a job,' murmured the doctor, and would have put a question had not Sergeant Mansell interrupted.

'The drowning case Gillen, by any chance?'

'Yes. I located his remains yesterday resting on dead Lake Otway. Man named MacLennon – you know him, perhaps – was struck by the sun. We were camped in the shadow of a hut, and I believe the heat upset him even before he determined to walk back to the out-station without a hat or a shirt. You can deal with the heat case on the spot, but the other two must be referred to a pathologist.'

'Ah-ha!' exclaimed the sergeant. 'Suspicious circumstances?'

'Yes.'

'As you will remember, Inspector, I was never satisfied about Gillen's disappearance, even before the money interest came out. Is this fire business mixed up with the Gillen affair?'

'It might be,' cautiously replied Bony, recalling that Mansell's first report on Gillen cast no doubts on accidental death. 'Is Draffin coming on behind us?'

'Yes. Loaded with stores and gear and stuff, including a coffin.'

'Did you bring a constable?'

'Too right, Inspector. He's travelling with Mr Wallace.'

'Good. Until the morning carry on as though everything is routine. Let no one suspect you think anything wrong in the case of Mrs Fowler. Tomorrow I will begin my inquiry into the deaths of Mrs Fowler and Raymond Gillen, following which you, Doctor, can with Sergeant Mansell decide your subsequent actions.'

'The fire victim is to be our first charge, Inspector?'

'Yes. On our arrival there will be much confusion till the place is put in order by Wallace and his men. The remains of Mrs Fowler, and the office safe, must not be tampered with until daylight.'

* * *

Confusion there was, and yet order was eventually established by Wallace. Barby was dispatched to Johnson's Well to transfer his camp and return the men's belongings. In the hearing of all, Doctor Clive said he would like to examine the body of MacLennon as quickly as possible, and that the remains of Mrs Fowler could be retrieved at daylight. That brought sobs from Joan, and Wallace himself took her to sit in the old arm-chair on the veranda.

Martyr went off with the doctor to Johnson's Well; Lester and Carney proceeded to build a camp fire and erect over it a beam from which Barby could suspend his billies and dixies. The fire illumined the front of the quarters and the line of out-buildings, and, when Draffin arrived, it aided the helpers to unload the stores and gear ... and the coffin, so handled that Joan did not see it.

With utensils Draffin brought from the main homestead, Lester brewed coffee, and opened tins of biscuits, meat and cheese. Oil-lamps were lit and Wallace took a large suit case to an empty room, then told Joan his wife had packed it for her. The room was next to that occupied by Lester.

Barby returned with his load, and at once washed and then took charge of the fire and the cooking. All the dogs were loosed, and the two cats cleaned themselves under Barby's feet and his galah in the cage woke to mutter words which disgraced its owner. With tragedy absent, it could have been a festive occasion.

A kind of buffet dinner was set out on a trestle table distant from the fire for comfort and yet advantaged by its light. They stood around to eat, and spoke in subdued tones because of the dead and the presence of Joan Fowler, now arrayed in a lime silk dress once packed in that suitcase.

Nothing about her registered the strain she had undergone for many hours. Firelight burnished the red-gold hair, and the silk dress gleamed as greenly as her eyes.

'What happened to you, Mr Martyr?' asked Carney when the chance offered.

'Had fan-belt trouble a mile this side of The Shaft,' replied the overseer. 'Spent a couple of hours messing about with it. Didn't get to Sandy Well till after eleven last night and then no one was in the office.'

'Don't wait up on the chance of hearing disaster on the phone,' remarked Wallace. 'Heard about it, of course, this morning. Mr Martyr wanted to return here, on a bit of rope for a fan-belt and a prayer. Just as well he didn't, with the heat rocking the mercury all over the States. Could easily have perished. As for us ... we left about five this afternoon, and even then the petrol almost exploded a dozen times before we got to Sandy Well.'

Lester came to sniffle and announce that the thermometer still registered 101 degrees, and when told by the sergeant of the record at Menindee he was as pleased as though he had backed a Melbourne Cup winner. Obviously he was trying to be cheerful ... as the others were ... and it did not appear that Joan ignored their efforts.

'We weren't to blame, Mr Wallace,' she entreated Wallace. 'Mother was always so careful with the stove and the frig. It was so quick, so sudden.'

'Try not to think about it too much, Joan,' advised the big man. 'We'll straighten it all out tomorrow. The place was old and the heat would make it tinder-dry. You did your best, and all of us can imagine how quickly it happened.'

Reaction set in and she burst into tears. Martyr stared hard at Barby's fire. Carney turned his back on her and sipped coffee. It was Lester who gently patted her shoulder. Wallace looked meaningly at the doctor, and Clive nodded. She did, however, insist on helping Barby to clean up.

It was not unusual for the 'government house' party to camp apart from the men, and Red Draffin put up stretchers for Wallace and the doctor, the sergeant and Martyr outside the store which was the closest to the site of the burned homestead. The men gathered in the light given from the cooking fire, and presently Red Draffin joined them.

He was barefoot as usual, his trousers and shirt were greasy and stained, as usual. And, as usual, his face was enlivened by his smile and twinkling eyes. Joan happened to be in her room.

'How did the rabbits go, George?' was his first question, and Barby glowered.

'Still going,' he answered, carefully stepping over a cat. 'Fenced the Channel yesterday. This morning the Channel is yards under dead rabbits and 'roos and birds.'

'I oughta been with you.'

'No good. The 'roos tore the fence down, and the sun did the rest. There'll be millions of rabbits digging under the dead uns to get at the water this very minute.' The glower lifted, the dark eyes cleared. Triumph crept into Barby's voice. 'But we needn't worry about the rabbits. A bit of a heat-wave can't knock them out. There'll be millions get through this summer, and when she rains they'll breed like hell. You ever seen a picture of the mouse licking up the drops of wine leaking from a barrel, and the cat's sitting on the top step of the cellar? The mouse says: "Now where's that bloody cat?" And that's what all the rabbits will be saying, Red: "Now where's that bloody myxotocksis?" '

24

Inspector Bonaparte Works

AFTER BREAKFAST, eaten before sun-up, everyone went into action, determined to accomplish as much as possible before the intense heat once again singed the earth and them. By nine o'clock the heat was severe, but a high-level haze smoked the sky and forecast a change accompanied by wind.

Sergeant Mansell and his constable appeared much interested in the interior of the machinery shed, whilst the others, including the owner and the overseer, relaxed on the veranda of the quarters.

Then the constable crossed to the group on the veranda to address Bony:

'Sergeant would like a few words with you.'

The general conversation petered out as Bony accompanied the policeman to the machinery shed. The doors were wide, the roof was high, the temperature was not yet unbearable. Packing-cases had been placed to form a desk and serve as seats, and the sergeant was taking from his brief-case paper, pens and ink.

'This do, Inspector?' he asked a little stiffly.

'Yes. We'll sit, so. As we deal with each of these people they must be kept here, not allowed to circulate. We'll begin with Carney. All right, Constable. Produce Henry Carney.'

Like those who were to follow him, Carney received a succession of surprises. He was surprised by finding Bony sitting with Mansell behind the 'desk', and was surprised by the invitation to sit on a tea-chest before them. Carney had been told that the sergeant wanted a few words with him, therefore the culminating surprise came when Mansell said:

'This is Inspector Bonaparte, Harry. He wants to ask a few questions.'

'Concerning Raymond Gillen, Mr Carney,' Bony said smoothly. 'We won't waste time by going into what is general knowledge but keep to essentials.'

Carney stared, knew he stared. The easy-going, softly-spoken horse-breaker had undergone a remarkable metamorphosis, for he sat squarely, his eyes were deeply blue, and there was no trace of the previous reticence of the aboriginal part of him. The voice was precise and authoritative.

'Mr Carney. Did you ever have a serious disagreement with Raymond Gillen?'

'No. Never,' answered Carney, barely side-stepping the 'sir'.

'What was your feeling towards Gillen?'

'Friendly enough. We got on all right. Camped in the same room. Most of us liked him. I know I did.'

'Despite the fact that you were both in love with the same girl?'

'That's only partly true. Ray wasn't in love with Joan. He thought he had a chance, that's all.'

'You were in love with her, were you not?'

'Yes. I was, then.'

'You imply you are not in love with her now. Would you tell me what changed your feelings?'

'That had nothing to do with Gillen,' prevaricated Carney. 'Gillen was a good type. Dare anything; try anything. He had a try for Joan, and it didn't upset me because I thought he would never get her. I know what she is. Yes, I loved her and hoped she'd marry me. I knew that Gillen meant to buy her, and I knew that because Gillen told me, and showed me money enough to buy a dozen women. It was in his case ... rolls and rolls of it.'

'Did he tell you where he obtained the money?'

'Spun a yarn about winning it in a lottery.'

'Do you know what happened to the money?'

'No.'

'You will remember that when MacLennon was shown the locket belonging to Gillen, he became enraged and said that Gillen had left a letter in his suitcase which you had found. Was that true?'

'Yes,' replied Carney. 'I'll tell you what happened from the time Ray had been here about a month. We'd become good friends, and he knew I was keen to marry Joan. He asked me, and I told him straight. He asked what I thought of my chances, and I said they were good ... until he came to the Lake. He said "Look, Harry. Don't be a mug. You've got no money and that's all she's after. She's a teasing bitch." '

Carney's mouth was grim, and his brown eyes were empty of the laughter Bony so often had seen.

'I knew what Ray said was right,' he went on. 'And then he said if I gave away the idea of marrying Joan, he'd give me a hundred to get her out of my system. When I laughed at him about the hundred, he opened his case and told me to help myself. He said again he'd won it in a lottery, but I couldn't believe that. But he did offer me a hundred to work off on Joan. I wouldn't take it. But I thought a hell of a lot of Ray Gillen.

'Then one night Joan said she wanted to go for a walk. She told me that Gillen had a case full of notes, and that he must have pinched it, and she wasn't being mixed up with hot money. She said she'd marry me if I stole it from Gillen, because then Gillen couldn't do anything about it, as he stole it in the first place. That woke me up to her properly. I didn't hate her exactly. I still loved her, or what I thought she could be. I still love her that way. I'm sorry if I can't make you understand.'

'I do understand,' Bony said slowly. 'Go on.'

'It turned out that Gillen got to work on her, offering her a thousand quid to clear out with him on his bike. She wouldn't fall for it. So he raised the ante ... just like he would. She said she didn't believe his yarns, and so he took her to his room and opened his case for her to see for herself.

'D'you know what, Bony? Joan planned to get all that money for free. She told her mother about it, and then the mother sooled MacLennon to steal it for her. Mac must have thought it over, and must have tried to open Gillen's case, because Ray found marks on the locks.

'Four days after that, or four nights after, Ray went for his last swim. Or so it turned out. When he wasn't on hand the next morning I looked at his case. It wasn't locked. Instead of the money, there was a letter. And the letter read: "What you want isn't here. It's well planted, and the clue is inside the locket around my neck. Try for the locket if you have guts enough. Ray G."

'I thought one of them had murdered Gillen, for the money. I don't think so now, not after you opened the locket for everyone to see.'

'Did Gillen tell you he was going to plant the money?'

'No. Not a word.'

'What did you do with the letter?'

'I gave it to Joan for a birthday present,' Carney grimaced. 'She didn't even thank me.'

'Did Gillen write letters?'

'No. He told me his parents were dead.'

'Did he seem to be worried ... just before the night he disappeared?'

'No. I've been trying to tell you what Gillen was, a chap who feared nothing, and no one. He never lost his temper.'

'He did fight Mac. Why?'

'Over what he said about Ma Fowler. But he didn't lose his temper about it. Mac did, and got a hell of a thrashing. Gillen laughed all the time he was dealing it out.'

'Let us return to the suitcase. The rooms are small, and each contains two beds. You camped with Gillen in the same room. When on your bed could you see Gillen's case under his?'

'At times. Depended on how far he pushed it under.'

'Quite so. When you could see the case, it was invariably locked?'

'The locks were in place and the catches were up. By looking at the case, I wouldn't know if the key had been turned in the lock.'

'When did you first find the case unlocked?'

'That morning Gillen was missing. I sat up and found Ray wasn't in his bed. I could see his suitcase under the bed. The ordinary catches weren't in place, and the slides were open. In fact the lid wasn't closed properly. That's why I pulled the case out and looked for the money, and found the letter.'

'In an envelope?'

'No. Just folded three times. It was lying on top of the clothes.'

Bony lit a cigarette.

'You have been candid, Mr Carney. Now tell me why you did not hand that letter to Mr Martyr, or to Sergeant Mansell.'

'I thought it might be a forgery, put in the case by whoever had taken the money, and could have murdered Gillen. I decided I'd stand by and wait to see who left here, and then

I'd have the satisfaction of reporting it to the police. But no one left the place.'

From the floor at his feet, and hidden by the cases from Carney, Bony picked up the parcel of money.

He was satisfied by Carney's reactions that Carney did not know its contents, but he asked the question:

'Have you seen this parcel before?'

Carney shook his head, and was directed to relax on the row of cases placed along one wall of the shed.

'Produce Robert Lester.'

The constable disappeared. The sergeant lit his pipe. He was the senior officer of a police-controlled district, and yet refrained from asking questions of the man who could give orders like that.

Lester sniffled before he came on. On seeing Bony, he sniffled again, and for the third time when told to sit on the tea-chest. On being informed that Inspector Bonaparte wished to ask a few questions, his watery eyes dried up. The bright blue eyes were expectant, and he knew there was a trap baited to take him, and wished he were far, far away.

Nonchalantly Bony removed the trap and placed it on the ground at his feet ... the parcel of money. He reached for pencil and paper and drew a sketch of the front of the men's quarters, the while Lester sharply watched him, the sergeant curious, and the audience of one, Carney. Then the voice so different from the easy drawl of the horse-breaker:

'Now, Mr Lester, tell me: do you sleep soundly at night?'

'Fairish, I think,' replied Lester.

'Do you sleep soundly in the daytime?'

'Caw! Hell of a hope sleepin' in daytime. I can't answer that one, Bony.'

The sergeant coughed disapprovingly at such *lèse-majesté*.

'You remember that afternoon when you were feeling off colour following a nightmare in which you were climbing in and out of a tank? You were awakened by Miss Fowler and told the house was on fire. You were having a nap on the veranda, remember? Were you sound asleep then?'

'Must have been. Never heard the fire; leastways, I thought it was a willi-willi passing by.'

'You had lunch at the usual time ... half-past twelve. After lunch you returned to the quarters. Who served the lunch?'

'Joan.'

'Did you see Mrs Fowler?'

'No.'

'Did you hear Mrs Fowler talking in the kitchen, or moving about in the kitchen?'

Lester proved that he had indulged in retrospection.

'Not a sight or sound of her.'

'After lunch, did you dally at table talking with Miss Fowler?'

'No. She seemed in a bit of a temper.'

'With whom? You? Her mother?'

'Didn't let on.'

'So that you must have left the kitchen after lunch at about one o'clock?'

'Yair. Musta been.'

'What did you do after leaving the annexe?'

'Went over to the quarters. I had a smoke, and wanted a paper to read, but there wasn't any and so I made meself comfortable and took a nap.'

'Would you say you were asleep before one-thirty?'

'I would,' answered Lester, adding confidently: 'And by the shadders I'd say it was just before two when I was awoke by Joan to see the ruddy house going up.'

'Thank you! Now look at this sketch of the quarters showing the room doors, the steps up to the veranda.' Bony rose and passed round to stand beside Lester. 'Was the old armchair about here?'

'She was. Yes, that's about where she was. Always is, remember?'

'I should do, Mr Lester. Was the back of the chair towards the steps?'

'Yair.'

'Would the door of the sitting-room be, say, ten feet from the chair?'

'About that, I reckon.'

'Then the back of the chair would be sixteen to twenty feet from the door to your room?'

'Yair. That's so.'

'And even if you had been awake, you would not have seen anyone move up the steps, walk across the veranda and enter your room?'

'I might have heard 'em.'

'But you were asleep.'

'Dead to the wide, matter of fact.'

'Right!' snapped Bony. 'See that brown paper parcel?'

'Yair,' assented Lester, staring at the trap brought up from the floor.

'What was it doing under your bed after the fire?'

'Search me.' Lester was plainly puzzled, and Bony was satisfied.

'Thank you, Mr Lester. Please join Mr Carney.'

He slouched away to sit with Carney. He sniffled before automatically biting a chew from a plug. He sniffled when Bony said:

'Produce Richard Martyr.'

25

Telling Tales

MARTYR SAT ON the tea-chest. He looked to Sergeant Mansell. The light-grey eyes, invariably in startling contrast with his complexion, were almost lazy until the sergeant said that Inspector Bonaparte wanted to ask questions. When Bony looked up from his notes, the pale-grey eyes were small, and the firm, determined mouth was small, and there was a paleness about the small nostrils.

'Mr Martyr, what time did you leave the homestead on the morning of the fire?'

'Ten past eight.'

'You did not return until after the fire, accompanied by Carney?'

'No. We saw the smoke plume from Winters Well ... sixteen miles away.'

'I was here with Barby, Lester and Miss Fowler when you returned with Carney after the fire. You gave instructions to the effect that we were to accompany Barby to Johnson's Well, and remain there until you returned from reporting the fire to Mr Wallace. You left before we did. When you had passed over the first ridge, you stopped the utility, watched the out-station to see us depart for Johnson's Well, and then you returned to the out-station. Why?'

'I did not return from beyond the first ridge.'

'You did. Your tracks betrayed you.'

'All right! I remembered that the Boss would ask me did I look into the safe to see if the books had been destroyed. I ought to have done it before I left. The stock books and records are important, and the Boss would be anxious about them.'

'You opened the safe and found the books ... in what condition?'

'Fairly good, to my relief.'

'What did you do then?'

'I locked the safe and carried on.'

'Leaving the key in the lock?'

'I ...' Martyr automatically touched the pockets of his jodhpurs.

'Must have done. Damn!'

'What else is in the safe besides the books?'

'Oh, tax stamps, a few pounds in petty cash.'

'Do you customarily carry the safe key in your pockets when you leave the out-station?'

Those pale-grey eyes stood by their owner.

'No. Usually it's kept on a little nail in the wall behind the desk.'

'And yet a little while ago when the key was mentioned you unconsciously tapped your pockets.'

'Why not? I remembered I took the key from the safe that morning and pocketed it because I was in a hurry.'

'Of course, Mr Martyr. Obviously the contents of the safe were of such great value that you would not habitually carry the key in a pocket when out on the run. The books found not to be seriously damaged, forgetting to relock the safe and remove the key is understandable. To replace the safe and cover it with ash is, however, curious. Well, now, I don't think there is anything else.'

Martyr rose and strode to the open door. Bony called:

'Oh, just a moment, Mr Martyr. Won't keep you long.'

Martyr turned, walked back to the desk. There he stood looking down at the brown-paper parcel Bony was holding.

From the parcel, his eyes flickered to encounter the blue eyes from which he couldn't hide. Actually, Bony was a little surprised when Martyr sat down.

'Where did you find that?' he asked, thinly.

'In Lester's room.'

'Lester's room!' echoed the overseer. Then came the one word, loudly: 'When?'

'After the fire . . . after.'

Martyr placed his elbows on the desk and cupped his chin in his hands. He put a question to the sergeant:

'Have I got to tolerate this inquisition?'

'No, there's no compulsion, Mr Martyr,' replied Mansell. 'Would look bad if you refuse, of course.'

'Yes, I suppose it would.' Martyr removed his gaze from the grey eyes to the bright blue eyes, and the blue eyes detected neither fear nor despair, but resolution.

'I don't like answering questions,' Martyr said sharply. 'I'm used to asking them. Do you know what's in that parcel?'

'Money. Shall I tell the story, or would you care to?'

'I will. I can tell it better than you. Two days before Gillen vanished, he came to the office after dark and requested me to take custody of a parcel which, he said, contained personal effects he treasured. I consented to do so, saying I would place the parcel in the station safe. I told him I would write a receipt for the parcel, and he laughed and said that wasn't necessary. I waxed the knots and at one place got him to press his thumb.

'I didn't think anything more of the parcel until, on the phone, Mr Wallace told me to run through Gillen's effects to establish his connexions, and when I opened the parcel I was astounded to see the large amount of money it contained.

'Not having found anything among Gillen's effects leading to his parents or friends, or where he came from, and feeling sure he could not possibly have gained the money by honest means, I decided to forget about the parcel in the safe. I realized that it mightn't do to resign right away and start off on my own, but that I must be patient and wait on here, perhaps for several years. My mother is almost an invalid, and I am her only support. I was able to send her a few pounds now and then together with a salary cheque.

'Naturally, when the house burned down, I was anxious

about the parcel, and you know that when I got here the safe would have been too hot to touch, and I didn't want the men to see me interested too much in it. Which is why I ordered them to go with Barby to his camp. So I returned, as you said, and opened the safe, and took the parcel to Lester's room, intending to retrieve it on my return and before I went to Johnson's Well for the men. It was my intention to steal the money. I believed Gillen had stolen it, or that it was stolen money, so that my action didn't seem to be so bad.'

'H'm!' Bony added a note to his pad. 'Having taken the parcel from the safe, you forgot to take the key. You threw ash on the safe and over your tracks as you withdrew from the ruins. Then you took the parcel to Lester's room and hid it under the mattress on Lester's bed. Why? Why didn't you take the parcel with you? You were in no possible danger of being searched.'

'I couldn't be sure I would not have to take over another ute, or drive Mr Wallace's car. And having lost everything bar what I stood up in in the fire, possession of the parcel might have been noticed.'

'Didn't you think that Lester might return from Johnson's Well, and might have found the parcel under the mattress?'

'No. Anyway, that was a chance I had to accept.'

'Yes, of course.' Bony regarded the overseer for a long moment. 'I think, Mr Martyr, I could tell the story better than that. Just where did you hide the parcel in Lester's room?'

'Where? Under the mattress, as I stated.'

'Think! Think, man!'

Martyr reddened with anger.

'If you didn't find it under the mattress, then someone found it before you. That's where I put it.'

'I rode back from Johnson's Well, and saw the dust raised by your utility after your second departure,' Bony went on. 'After you left for the second time, and before I arrived here, there was certainly no other person in sight. Therefore, no one could have removed the parcel from under the mattress, because it was never under the mattress.'

'All right! Then where was it?'

'You don't know, Mr Martyr?'

'Under the mattress was where I put it.'

'I repeat, Mr Martyr, you don't know where I found the

parcel, because you did not hide the parcel in Lester's room.'

'I tell you I did. And my word is as good as yours.'

Bony bent over and brought to view the station books.

'See the slight damage done these books by the heat in the safe, generated outside the safe. The covers are brittle. Here are the tax stamps, curled by the heat to thin spills. Now regard the parcel of money. The wrapping does not bear any such effects of heat. So, Mr Martyr, the parcel was taken from the safe before the fire . . . when you were miles away on a job with Carney.'

Martyr said nothing, looking at Bony, trying to evade the ice-blue eyes, being compelled to face them again and again.

'You returned from just beyond the first ridge,' Bony continued. 'You opened the safe to remove the parcel, which already had been taken, and you began then to guess about the fire, and you knew who took the parcel from the safe before the fire began. And those questions you asked yourself, and hated to answer, because you don't like answering questions, are questions I have asked myself, and have supplied the answers. Nothing you can say will affect the result to the person who removed the parcel of money from the office safe. I suggest that you concentrate on Gillen.'

The only sound within the shed was the occasional creaking of the roof iron tortured by the sun. Martyr bit his lip, and then his finger-nails. Bony rolled a cigarette. Sergeant Mansell stared at the overseer and was glad he wasn't the object of this suavely polite interrogation. Martyr sighed, moved to roll himself a smoke, as though to steady his fingers. His voice was flat.

'I was sitting on the house veranda. The moon was full. It was late, after eleven. I saw Gillen walk down to the water. He was wearing only pyjama trousers and once the moonlight was reflected by the golden locket suspended from his neck.

'He ran into the water, and then he splashed it over himself, as he continued to run, getting deeper and deeper until he lunged forward and began to swim. For some time I could see his dark head on the silvered water and watch the outward-running ripples under the moon. Presently, he swam from my sight, swam on towards the far shore.

'I sat on the veranda, thinking. Then I heard a cry. It was

far out on the Lake. At first I thought it was Gillen playing the fool. Then I heard, low but distinctly, his cries for help, including the word "cramp". I did not get up. I knew Gillen wasn't playing the fool, but I didn't get up from the chair. I sat on and listened to Gillen drowning.

'You must understand why I hated Gillen, and why I let him drown.

'Living conditions here were rough before Mrs Fowler and her daughter were employed. But, life was smooth for all of us. I had my first big job. The men were easy to get along with. There was no clashing and no unpleasantness. The women changed all that. They brought order and cleanliness and decent living, but they also brought hate and pain.

'That was three years ago, and I thought Joan was innocent and sweet as well as beautiful. I asked her to marry me. She said she would like to think about it. I took her riding, gave her little presents. She asked me how I stood financially. I told her I hadn't been able to save because I had to support my mother. I offered her the partnership in my job here, and was confident one day of becoming a full manager. She said she wouldn't marry a man in my position and with my prospects. The man she married must be rich. When I pressed her, she told me I was too dull, and too old, anyway.

'That was before Gillen came. Carney was trying his luck when Gillen asked for a job. I used to watch the play. I was asked by this one and that to obtain a wages cheque from the Boss, and then when making up the mail I'd see a letter addressed to a Sydney or an Adelaide jeweller. I became satisfied to wait, and bet with myself which of the men would finally murder her.

'Gillen came and he fancied Joan, and Joan seemed to fall for him. Gillen must have been fifteen years younger than I am. In modern parlance, he had everything it takes. She played with me, and she played with Carney, but she meant business with Gillen ... until she came to me one evening and was sweet and loving and told me that Gillen had a lot of stolen money in his suitcase. She suggested that I take it, saying it must have been stolen by Gillen, and what was stolen would not be real stealing the second time. And that when Gillen discovered his money was gone he wouldn't dare make a fuss about it, and we could go away and be married and start with plenty of cash. The Golden Bitch! I told her to use someone else.

'The very next night, Gillen came to me with the money in a parcel, and after he had gone back to the quarters, I opened the parcel, made sure that it contained a fortune in bank-notes, and retied and resealed it and put it in the safe.

'I stayed on the veranda a full two hours after I heard Gillen shouting for help from the middle of the Lake, and by then was sure he had drowned. Because all the time he'd been here he had never written a letter, but had signed the employees' work-book, I imitated his handwriting and wrote a note saying he had planted his money and that the clue to the plant was in his locket and daring anyone to take the locket from him. I knew someone had been after the money, because Gillen told me his case had been tampered with.

'At four in the morning the front of the quarters was in deep shadow, and I took the note and crept into Gillen's room and put it into the case. If someone came after the money and took the note, they'd be ready to get in first for the locket when the body came ashore. And if by chance it didn't, they'd have to wait for the Lake to dry up. If no one opened the case, I'd give the note to Joan for the pleasure of seeing her reaction. But when I listed the contents of the case, the note was gone, and as Gillen's body didn't turn up, I sat back and watched the play go on.'

'Who knew where the safe key was normally kept?' asked Bony.

'No one other than Mr Wallace and myself.'

'And on the morning of the first you inadvertently left the key in the safe lock?'

'I did. That morning when Mr Wallace rang through he wanted stock figures and I had to refer to the stock book. I forgot to relock the safe. That is the story, Inspector. I have nothing to add to it. I shall continue to sit back and watch the play, because I know now that you know the end of it.'

26

Who Wins?

JOAN APPEARED, escorted by the constable, and behind them came Mr Wallace, who had been requested by Bony not to leave the poor girl alone to brood.

She looked cool and confident in a lilac dress and sling-back sandals. Her hair was gloriously, vividly alive and her make-up was, as usual, lightly applied. She gave Bony a tender smile and then concentrated on Sergeant Mansell, who had sent word that he wished to ask questions. It was when Bony was presented as Inspector Bonaparte that she froze.

'You, a detective-inspector!'

'When I am not breaking-in horses, yes. Now be easy, Miss Fowler. I just want you to tell us about the fire so that this matter of your mother's unfortunate end may be cleared up. Would you tell Sergeant Mansell just what happened?'

'What, again?' Joan tossed her hair, settled herself on the hard tea-chest, and related her experience as previously given to Bony and others.

'Thank you,' murmured Bony. 'Let us be quite clear. Your mother was lying down on her bed. She occupied a room other than yours?'

'Yes. When I ran to her she was lying on her bed and I tried to wake her up and couldn't. So I pulled her off the bed and tried to drag her from the room, but the fire and smoke was too much for me, and I just got out myself. As I told you.'

'When you first noticed the fire, you were lying down on your own bed?'

'Yes.'

'Fully dressed, of course?'

'Oh, yes. I had had a shower and dressed for the afternoon. I was reading a book when I saw smoke pouring into my room and then I heard the crackle of the flames.'

'It was, if memory serves, a very hot afternoon, Miss Fowler. You would have found the shade cast by the garden trees much cooler. During the morning you swept out the office, I understand.'

'No. I didn't. Mother did, I think.'

'Supposing you tell us about the money in the unlocked safe.'

'Money in the safe!' echoed Joan. 'What are you talking about?'

'This money,' replied Bony, and brought up the parcel to place it on the desk. 'Gillen's money. It was in the safe before the house caught fire. It was not in the safe when the house was burning. After the house burned to ash, it was in Lester's room ... under his bed and pushed as far back as possible. Can you tell us anything concerning this strange angle?'

'I still don't know what you are talking about!' persisted the girl, her eyes indignant, but voice controlled.

'You knew, of course, that Gillen possessed a great deal of money, and that everyone thought he had stolen it?'

'It's the first I've heard of it. And if you believe tales told you by Harry and Mr Martyr about me, you're a fool. They're spiteful liars. They've always been sore because I wouldn't give in to them. This has never been a safe place for a decent girl, but Mother and I had to live, and we could save something from our wages.'

'These tales about you have to be checked, you know,' Bony said soothingly. 'It's my job. Let's return to the fire. Of course, you know there will have to be an inquest, and it's better to have it all straightened out for the coroner. Would you prefer to sign a statement covering your actions from the time you realized the house was on fire?'

'Yes, I would.'

Bony wrote down the details.

'There you are. Please read it carefully before you sign it. Then we'll witness your signature, and make it hard and fast.'

The girl read the document. She picked up the pen provided by Mansell. She looked at Bony, who was rolling a cigarette. She glared at Martyr and Carney, who had drawn close at Bony's beckoning.

'That is what happened,' she said. 'Every word of it. I don't tell lies about people.'

With angry deliberation she wrote her name, and sat

back while Carney and Martyr and Lester witnessed her signature.

'You might confirm the document, Mr Wallace,' suggested Bony, and Wallace signed as a Justice of the Peace. The men were waved away, and Bony continued. 'Now that subject is covered, Miss Fowler, let us make clear the subject of your mother's jewellery.'

Bony thought to make the girl betray shock, and when he saw no evidence of it he could not but wonder at the manifestation of a one-track mind, unable to anticipate a trap. Here was a woman so sure of her power, made so vain by her victories, that even the subject of her mother's jewellery did not, at this moment, disturb her, as she deftly renewed her make-up.

'Well, what about Mum's bits and pieces?' she demanded, slipping the gold compact into the pocket of her skirt. Bony smiled ruefully, saying:

'I find this as irritating as you must do, Miss Fowler. Do you remember Lester giving your mother a gold brooch set with opals?'

'Yes. She showed it to me when Lester gave it to her.'

'Did you see the emerald ring given your mother by MacLennon?'

'Yes.'

'And the pendant?'

'Yes. Why all this?'

'Where did your mother usually keep her jewellery?'

'Oh, I don't know. Never interested that much.'

'Do you think she would keep her jewellery in an old handbag behind the door of the ladies' tante?'

'Tante! What's tante?'

'Aunt.' The girl laughed, and Bony said suavely:

'Constable, take Mr Wallace and Mr Lester to the room now occupied by Miss Fowler, and bring here any jewellery you may find.'

The girl jumped to her feet and stormed, her voice harsh, her words raw. The sergeant stood and towered over her. The constable and Lester departed, the mystified Mr Wallace following after them. Bony glanced across at the two men again seated by the wall. Martyr was leaning back and resting his head against a wall support. His eyes were closed, and he was smiling. Carney sat tensely, his eyes wide, as horror strangled an ideal which had striven to live.

'Sit down, Miss, and keep calm,' urged Mansell. 'The Inspector's only getting things straightened out.' She looked up at him searchingly, her hands clenched. Abruptly she turned to Bony. Bony was writing a memo, and she sat again and from the cigarette section of the gold compact she extracted a smoke. The sergeant struck a match for her. She inhaled clumsily, and as she spurted smoke through pursed lips, Bony looked up and the light in his eyes caused her to flinch.

'You don't know where Gillen planted his money, do you?' he asked, softly. 'I do. I know how his money came to be in Lester's room, and who conveyed it thereto. I know why it was hidden under Lester's bed. And I know who took your mother's jewellery to the tante, before the fire, and who removed it from the tante just before we all left for Johnson's Well. Greed is a loathsome vice, Miss Fowler. Beauty is a wonderful gift which should make the recipient deeply humble. When beauty is allied with greed and a lust for power, beauty is as nothing. You, with your possession of beauty, with the addition of a little intelligence, might have created a world of happiness.'

'Clever, aren't you!'

Sadly, Bony looked into her green eyes, mocking, cold, empty. Wallace came into the shed. The constable entered with Lester. The constable put on the desk gold and gems which caught the hot light from without.

'Lester! Is that the brooch you gave to Mrs Fowler?'

'Yair, it is. And that's the ring that Mac gave her. And here's the necklet Harry gave her, too. Isn't it, Harry?'

Carney made no move from his seat against the wall, and Bony said:

'Would you like to make a statement telling how your mother died?'

'I signed it.'

'That one isn't quite accurate.'

'I'm signing no other statement,' the girl said, contemptuously tossing her cigarette butt on to Bony's papers.

'Very well, I'll tell you how she died, and what you did afterwards. The case is so simple and so clear that the best lawyers in the country would fail in your defence. There is only one point which eludes me, and it is not important, and that is whether you or your mother found the office safe with the key in its lock.

'For years there has rested on the top of the safe a brass figurine, and this morning it was found where the passage door of the office originally swung.

'The doctor is sure that your mother was killed by a blow from that figurine. He is confident that the Government pathologist will support his opinion, and further will agree with him that the body was dragged on its back for some distance to the bedroom where the fire partially consumed it. The fact that a dustpan has been found on the place where the office stood indicates that one of you went there to sweep out the office. And there murder took place over the parcelled money taken from the safe.

'You dragged your mother's body from the office, along the passage and so to her room. That was before lunch, and Lester would be expecting to hear the gong struck. You called him to lunch at the right hour, and afterwards you collected all your mother's jewellery, your own bank-book and what loose money there was, as well as your toilet aids, and hid them in the handbag behind the door of the ladies' tante, dropping a ring on the path as you went there or returned.

'You foresaw that after setting fire to the house you would escape with nothing save what you were wearing. You could wear your own jewellery but not that belonging to your mother, and what place more secure against men than that you selected?

'Doubtless you were a trifle upset by the body in the house. What to do with the brown-paper parcel containing some twelve thousand pounds? The jewellery you could eventually hide down inside your blouse and in your skirt pocket. But not the parcel. That was too large. You would have put it in the tante, but you could not be sure what Mr Martyr would decide about your immediate future. So you looked across to the quarters and saw Lester dozing with his back to the steps, and you stole over with the parcel, silently gained the veranda and slipped into Lester's room because it was the first room you came to.

'After the fire, you gained your way with Martyr, or

thought you did, to let you stay at the out-station, but when compelled to accompany the men to Johnson's Well for a space, you retrieved the loot you had put in the handbag and stuffed it down your blouse. The parcel, however, you could do nothing with because one of us at least would see it. So I found the parcel under Lester's bed within two hours after we left in Barby's utility, and Mr Wallace with the constable and Lester found your mother's jewellery in the room given you since yesterday.'

'In the suitcase my wife packed and I brought here for her,' supplemented Mr Wallace.

'Damn clever, eh?' commented Joan, calmly.

'Heavens, no, one hasn't to be clever with you,' replied Bony, pleasantly. 'You know, actually, you are extremely dumb. Just listen to this. This is what you said and what you signed before witnesses: "I found Mother unconscious from the smoke and I dragged her off the bed. I couldn't lift her. The smoke was getting my breath, and the room was full of flames. I dragged Mother by her feet to the doorway, then I had to leave her and rush out because the house was all on fire." That is what you stated, and signed as the truth.'

'Well, so what, cocky?'

'Come, come, Miss Fowler! You cannot really be as dumb as that. If you dragged your mother off the bed and then by the feet to the doorway, her body would have been found by police and doctor with its feet to the doorway. She was found with her head to the doorway, proving that you had dragged her body by the feet to that place from the passage. From the passage, Miss Fowler, not from the bed. That'll be all, Sergeant.'

* * *

'Just a little conference before I depart with the Boss,' Bony told Lester and Carney and Martyr, he having drawn them to the edge of the bluff overlooking the dreary depression.

'Much will depend on the Crown Prosecutor,' he went on, 'but I fancy he won't take action against either you, Martyr, or you, Carney. Martyr, don't let this episode in your life spoil it. There was no action you could have taken to rescue Gillen that night, for had there been a boat he couldn't have been reached in time. As for the money ... well ... with no one to claim it and a mother desperately ill, I believe I would have . . . thought about it.

'As for you, Harry, cling to your dreams and remember that what one woman kills another can resurrect. Tell me, who did trounce Bob when he climbed out of that tank?'

'MacLennon,' sighed Carney, and Lester sniffled twice.

'The fourth man there that night? Was it you, Martyr?'

'Yes. I was keeping watch from the creek bank.'

'Who prepared Gillen's bike for a get-away?'

'I did,' Carney said. 'I was fed up with the place and all. Then I thought how silly I'd be.'

'You would have been, and it would not have been like you. And had you attempted to ride away after I came here, you would have found that the carburettor had been removed. We won't say anything more about Gillen's motor-cycle and, unless the matter crops up, we'll say nothing of the accidental discharge of the shot-gun, Mr Martyr. What did happen that night?'

'The women had been nagging each other for days, and I ought to have anticipated a showdown,' Martyr replied. 'The gun was kept on the wall in the hall, and cartridges are about anywhere. I was in my room, and I heard them arguing. A moment or two later, I heard the gun-breech snapped shut. It was a sound I couldn't mistake, and I raced to Joan's room and was just in time to push up the barrel of the gun as the mother pulled the trigger. I didn't make a song and dance about it, Inspector, as it would have spoiled my star act.'

'Yes, it would have been an anticlimax,' agreed Bony. He gripped Lester's forearm. 'Now, Bob, you cannot gossip without stones crashing through your windows. Remember, you have lived in a glass house. Imagine giving a woman a brooch worth £120 merely on a promise. Imagine what people would say. It made the gamble frightfully expensive, didn't it?'

'Yair, I suppose it did.' Lester forgot to sniffle, but he did chuckle. 'Still, if a bloke never gambles, he can't ever win, can he?'

'That's quite true, Bob,' agreed Bony, smiling. 'Yet when it comes to gambling on a woman, no man can win . . . ever. Now I must go. *Au revoir*, and grand luck for you all. Should you be here at the time, let me know when Lake Otway is born again.'

[illegible] a gambler desperately. [illegible] believe I would [illegible]

[illegible] as for you, Harry, [illegible] your speech and I remember just what [illegible] woman [illegible] another can [illegible] surface [illegible] when he climbed out of that tank."

[illegible] Carney, and Lester sniffed twice.

"The fourth man [illegible] here that night? Was it you, Marty?"

"Yes, I was keeping watch from the creek bank."

[illegible] Ollie's offer for a get-away [illegible]

[illegible] said [illegible] Harp with the plate and all. [illegible] how [illegible] he."

[illegible] would not have been [illegible] attempted [illegible] away after I came here, [illegible] would have [illegible] the [illegible] had been removed [illegible] anything more about Ollie's [illegible] and [illegible] well say nothing of the accidental [illegible] of the shotgun, Mr Marty. What did happen that night?"

"The women had been nagging each other [illegible] and I ought to have anticipated a showdown," Marty replied. "[illegible] kept on the wall in the hall, and cartridges [illegible] anywhere. I was in my room, and I heard them arguing. A [illegible] or two later, I heard the gun-breech snap. [illegible] I couldn't [illegible] Lester [illegible] raced to Lester's room [illegible] in time to push up the barrel of the gun as [illegible] pulled the trigger. I didn't make [illegible] and [illegible] Inspector, as it would have spoiled [illegible]"

[illegible] it would have been an unfortunate [illegible] Lester's [illegible]. Now [illegible] you [illegible] with [illegible] through your windows. Remember, [illegible] have [illegible] home, imagine giving a woman a [illegible] merely on a [illegible] to imagine what people would [illegible] the [illegible] expensive, [illegible]

[illegible] I suppose [illegible] did Lester forget to [illegible], but he did [illegible] of a [illegible] gambler he can't ever win.

[illegible] Bony [illegible] when it comes [illegible] gambling [illegible] Now [illegible] and [illegible] what [illegible] the [illegible] know when Lake Otway is [illegible]

PERCH [illegible]

DEATH OF A LAKE